THE
HUMMINGBIRDS

THE HUMMINGBIRDS

A NOVEL

ROSS MCMEEKIN

Skyhorse Publishing

Skyhorse Publishing books may be purchased in bulk at special discounts for sales promotion, corporate gifts, fund-raising, or educational purposes. Special editions can also be created to specifications. For details, contact the Special Sales Department, Skyhorse Publishing, 307 West 36th Street, 11th Floor, New York, NY 10018 or info@skyhorsepublishing.com.

Skyhorse® and Skyhorse Publishing® are registered trademarks of Skyhorse Publishing, Inc.®, a Delaware corporation.

Visit our website at www.skyhorsepublishing.com.

10 9 8 7 6 5 4 3 2 1

Library of Congress Cataloging-in-Publication Data is available on file.

Cover design by Erin Seaward-Hiatt
Cover Photograph: iStock

Print ISBN: 978-1-5107-2876-9
Ebook ISBN: 978-1-5107-2877-6

Printed in the United States of America

For Jess

For beauty is nothing but the beginning of terror
which we are barely able to endure, and it amazes
us so,
because it serenely disdains to destroy us.
                                          —Rainer Maria Rilke

ZERO

The pistol butt struck Ezra Fog's skull and the night stars smeared. Ezra reached out for balance. It was no use; his whirling mind couldn't hold still. He stumbled, blacked out, and fell overboard.

Moments later, he woke submerged in the cold silence of the ocean, nose and mouth filled with salt water. He choked and kicked through the muted darkness toward what he hoped was air until finally, body furious, mind in hysterics, he broke the surface. He coughed and spat and his starving lungs fought for breath. Iridescent lights flared about his vision. His left temple burned. His fingers felt for the ache and winced at the tender knot.

He gathered himself and treaded water. Slowly his mind recovered some measure of sense, and with it, his vision cleared enough for him to spot the rowboat, already a dozen yards away, sliding farther into the dark.

He felt ill. He retched up seawater. Swells moved through him as he again struggled to catch his breath. Once the dizziness passed and the stars flickering above settled back into place, all that had happened came back. It had been a fair fight, and he'd

been winning, and now he was alone, two miles out in the cold
Pacific, dim lights taunting him from shore. No one to blame
but himself.

He wiped his nose and what he felt was warm and smooth.
Blood. His throat tightened. In his imagination, the vast maw of
the sea opened below. Anything could be down there.

The boat was now only a jot on the horizon's script.

ONE

Nine Days Earlier

The first question that bloomed in Ezra's mind as he watched Sybil Harper crossing the patio was whether he'd done something wrong. But as he continued shearing the shrubs, that thought was replaced by a numb arousal. Beneath the hem of her canary-yellow robe strolled the legs that cynics claimed won her film roles; the pair the public loved to gaze at, celebrate, and demonize; the pair Ezra felt he had no right to lay eyes on, not simply because Sybil was married and a tenant, but because deep down he didn't feel he had the right to lay eyes on any woman at all.

He would turn thirty tomorrow and so little had changed.

She drew close, balancing a tray holding a highball on her palm. Her hair was aspen blonde, a single orchid set behind her ear. A royal knob rested in the bridge of her nose. And her eyes? Mercy. Not the massive, prepubescent globes of so many other actors, but bright blue shiners carefully guarded by her lids. Her eyes seemed weary, if weariness wasn't just sadness and regret but also irritation at having to show the world anything at all.

He rested the shears in the parched lawn and sat back on his haunches.

She gestured to the tray with her chin, as if to say *a drink, for you* without being bothered by words. He didn't know what to think. Or feel. This had never happened before, never a single interaction in the six months she'd lived in the rental property on the grounds he kept.

Except for that morning a couple of months back, if you could call it an interaction. He'd glanced out the pool house window to find her facedown in the prickly, rain-starved grass descending from the mansion, as if she'd been on her way to see him only to be struck by lightning. When he'd turned her over, she was blotto, face sallow, the front of her dress wrinkled and damp from sweat—a look that reminded him of the times he'd helped his mother through her own post-bender reckonings. He'd carried Sybil to a lawn chair in the patio, covered her in a patchwork collage of towels from the pool hutch, and left.

Sybil held out the drink.

"For me?" he asked.

She smiled. The recesses of her robe danced a little in the breeze, and he felt a slug of déjà vu. He'd seen this all before in at least a dozen forgettable movies. A fullness gripped his chest as he rose from his knees and took the glass. Behold, Sybil Harper. What he would do. What he wouldn't do. The porch. The pool. The flowerbed. Christ, the sod pile.

She fidgeted with the hem of her robe, along which trailed a vine of white flowers. He took a sip from the glass and felt the bite of alcohol on his tongue. He tried to think up something interesting to say, but failed. A breeze drifted through them, carrying a whiff of her shampoo or soap. He recognized the smell, something with coconut and cream, and it occurred to him that this vision in front of him was, in fact, real.

"Thank you," he said.

She pinched a few sprigs from a rosemary bush he'd been shaping and smelled. Her fingers were tan except for a pale line where a wedding band should have rested. Had she and her husband separated? He'd heard nothing in the tabloids. But he also hadn't seen Grant Hudson once in the time they'd lived there. Even before finding Sybil passed out on the lawn, Ezra had on occasion felt sorry for her as she wandered the grounds alone in the middle of the afternoon, absently tapping her phone. She was not the sort of person he'd ever imagined pitying.

He took a quick study of her face. The rims of her nose were a bit pink. Had she been crying? Her eyes seemed clear, and suddenly he realized that she was also appraising him.

Before he could respond, she gave a quick, wry smile and began walking back up to the mansion. Her arching ponytail fought the breeze while pointing down her softly tanned neck toward the bottom of her robe, which concealed her behind except for the brief, wicked moments when it grew taut and the form appeared.

He sank back down to his knees and a hummingbird zipped past, wings beating themselves invisible. The screen door closed with a clack. He took a deep breath. She had just made a pass at him. How could he call it anything else? Bryce wouldn't believe it. Neither would Maria. No one would believe it. He could scarcely believe it himself.

But no, that wasn't true. Bryce would believe it, because women made passes at Ezra all the time. Bryce would say something like *oh—shocking—the starlet wants someone on the side?* And sweet Maria, she would believe it too. She'd roll her eyes and laugh, and Ezra would laugh, because everyone knew that he wasn't that kind of guy, and because no one knew what kind of guy he actually was.

He sipped the spiked tea and took a deep breath. It was odd that Sybil had said nothing. If not for the drink, he might have wondered if it had been only his imagination. But maybe she felt about life the way he did—the less you said, the less you had to regret.

Through the corner of his eye, he thought he saw a drape shut on one of the eight-paneled windows on the second floor. He paused. No Sybil. Just the faux-sixteenth-century stone manor house winking at him. It loomed, all shoulders, like a cathedral holding forth in three stories of judgment.

Ezra finished the rest of the drink and walked across the checkered clay patio bordering the back entrance to the mansion. He set the empty glass next to the double doors and resumed pruning. As his shears opened and closed, he began composing a scene in his mind where he might have something to offer Sybil that she couldn't get from her big-shot husband and the rest of the mannequins around town.

And all morning, as Ezra pruned in the dry September heat, there was no relief from his desire. Nor did he seek any. He entertained it, and in doing so made the passing time feel less heartbreaking. In fact, so full was his escape that he failed to notice that he wasn't alone in his arousal. Everything around him was coital, from the midges jerking through the air with their abdomens conjoined, to the hummingbirds sticking their beaks in and out of the yellow-lobed lilies.

TWO

At dusk, Ezra began preparing a large dinner salad in the kitchen of the pool house where he lived. He washed celery stalks in the sink while a chlorinated breeze meandered through the unlatched window. Beyond, the mansion shielded the sunset and shadowed the tan grass, which yielded to groves of palms with flowers for moccasins. He allotted most of what little water the city granted for these tiny oases for hummingbirds.

He'd spent his lunch break with screen grabs of Sybil, partook, and now felt as he imagined the angels did: sexless. But it wasn't really the angels he wanted to feel like, it was his friend Bryce, who went to church every Sunday and made love to his girlfriend daily, without any qualms. Ezra's mother had often said in her sermons, *the most delicious fruit isn't the one you can't pluck, it's the one you shouldn't.* But Bryce treated words like *shouldn't* in the same way God seemed to treat his followers' expectations: with humor.

Ezra chopped celery into thin crescents, the dull knife struggling to punch all the way through the stalks. He glanced up. The grounds were quiet. The pool outside resembled a small group of concentric puddles. Evenings, it stayed lit and the water flickered as wind gusts caressed the surface—he'd photo-graphed it many times but could never quite capture the effect. He finished the celery and began rinsing spinach beneath the rush of water.

Ezra stopped. Something caught his eye, a movement out in the grounds. Someone? He waited for a moment, and another. Nothing. Maybe a bird or a cat. He continued washing the soft handful of spinach, then nearly dropped the leaves into the sink. Sybil stepped into the sparkling light near the pool, nude. Her pale white skin glowed aquamarine, illuminated from below by the submerged lamps. He could see a darkness between her legs and dancing light cupping her breasts.

His face tingled. When she'd been clothed he'd been aroused, but with her nude it felt overwhelming. He reached for his camera so he could hide behind its lens, but stopped: she looked straight at him and held his gaze. Could she see him? Yes. Shit. Rows of track lights glowed above the sink and the muted television flickered from the next room. Spinach crum-pled in his other palm.

While staring, Sybil dipped her toes into the pool, making no move to cover herself, as though she was daring him to keep watching while at the same time daring him to look away. The reflection of the blue water shimmered on her skin. Her beauty felt like a challenge, if not a threat. His eyes retreated to the sink and studied the salad he'd been preparing, as if it were some-how interesting, as if it weren't the same salad he'd prepared the night before, and the night before that.

A moment passed. He felt her gaze and became aware of his own anatomy. Every patch of dry skin, every scar, every mark, every hair that grew where he wished it wouldn't. How hideous it all might look. Any thoughts from that morning of how he might have something to offer her now felt absurd. Here he was, fully clothed, yet the one embarrassed.

He squatted and rustled around in the drawer beneath the sink, looking for something to justify his presence, but it all felt false in comparison to who stood outside the window.

He heard a splash and rose from his squat so that only his forehead and eyes breached the windowsill. Outside, Sybil's face and neck and shoulders emerged from the water, dripping, her hair lying flat and slick on her scalp. She slid both hands through it, fell forward, and began swimming laps.

This was someone else's wife, someone's *daughter*. Hadn't his mother often bludgeoned him with this perspective, even before a true thought of sex had entered his mind? He was tired, so tired of it all. He stood up and watched.

She swam. Her form wasn't graceful. She had a hitch in her left arm, and her legs were too bent. Something about that imperfection only intensified his feelings.

He stayed there watching. He felt the urge to pick up the DSLR camera resting on the counter, but resisted. As the evening grew, his face gradually appeared in the window, superimposed on the pool and the darkness beyond. A word rang in his mind: *pervert*.

But who, *who* could keep from looking at Sybil? Hadn't she built a career answering that question? Name the person who could avert their eyes and sign them up for sainthood. He picked up the camera and began snapping photographs of his reflection as it captured what it shouldn't.

Sybil stopped swimming, glided to the edge of the pool, and climbed out. He clicked pictures through every move. She rose and stood on the lip, once again facing Ezra. Dripping. Radiant. She dabbed her towel against her arms and face and pointed her toes as she slid her feet into her sandals. Pointed her toes? Unnecessary. Indulgent. Magnificent. Then, just before she left, she smiled.

Ezra felt a billowy rush of pleasure. His eyes strained to follow her shadowy form and soak up every last glimmer. Had she really smiled? Yes. Without a doubt. This was exactly what he'd feared and exactly what he'd hoped. He caught one more glimpse when she reached the patio—the motion sensor bulb flashed, lending enough light to paint a mirage in his mind of her body, fluorescent.

He remained by the window, water still running, crushed spinach pooling at the bottom of the sink. His phone buzzed. It was Bryce. They'd talked about getting a drink. It buzzed again. He let it go to voice mail.

Ezra set the camera down and his stomach announced its emptiness. He felt ravenous. This salad was a joke. He needed a steak soaked in butter, a sweet roll stuffed with brie and honey, a stream of chocolate fudge dripping down his chin and onto his chest. He flipped off the spigot, looked up, and saw a huge oriel window lit on the top floor of the mansion, a beacon glowing amber through drapes. He swore. And laughed. Sybil Harper wasn't just married; she was his de facto employer. And not only that, she inhabited a social class dozens of rungs above his own. No matter how much he desired her, no way. For a woman like Sybil to even make overtures was dangerous. If Grant Hudson discovered she was hitting on the groundskeeper? Pink slip and no recommendations.

It wasn't really a decision. Regardless of what all the other gardeners and nannies and maids and cabana boys did with movie stars, he would stay inside and pretend nothing happened. Not only would he keep his dignity, he'd preserve his employment and prevent a mess he hadn't asked for. Keep the peace, or whatever this was.

Still, he hated it. The bruised spinach pooling in the sink made him want to punch a hole in the wall. But he picked it up and forced it down his throat.

THREE

The next day, in that early part of the afternoon when the sun tried its best to wilt everything in its stare, Ezra picked weeds. Perspiration dripped from his chin, wetting the dry earth, as the Dodgers game chattered live through his headphones. He unearthed a thick dandelion cluster, glanced up at the mansion, and blinked. From the massive oriel window on the top floor, Grant Hudson waved, gestured for Ezra to wait, and disappeared.

This was strange. Ezra had never spoken to him before. As far as he knew, Hudson was unaware that he even existed. Was this about the previous night? Had he seen Ezra there in the window taking pictures of his wife?

Hudson strolled through the back door and patio to the lawn, wearing sockless brown loafers, beige shorts, and a dress shirt. His cranium resembled a helmet and part of his belt buckle was hidden beneath an intermediate overflow of gut.

"Greetings, Ezra." Hudson rubbed his hands together.

Ezra removed his headphones and gloves. "Mr. Hudson." He held out his hand to shake. He almost said *nice to meet you,* but didn't, just in case Hudson was under the assumption that they'd already met. "How are you today?"

"I'm well, thanks. Spent the last two weeks up in Vancouver shooting a miniseries. I don't get how people live up there. The weather is shit." He laughed, jowls quivering with each chuckle; its sound was gruff and trustworthy, a laugh that said *I'm in control, but don't worry, I'm benevolent.* For a quick moment Ezra wondered whether his own father might have laughed like that, might still be laughing like that.

"Welcome back," Ezra said.

"Believe me,"—Hudson rocked back on his heels and shielded his brow from the sun—"it's agreeable." He licked his lips and gazed over the grounds. The only sound besides the low hum of neighboring Weedwackers was the crackled play-by-play of the baseball game leaking from the headphones wrapped around Ezra's neck.

Hudson gestured toward the expanse of lawn and they strolled. "Are you in the business?"

"No, sir." Ezra was often asked some version of that. And when people wouldn't ask, they'd stare. As he walked down the sidewalk. As he fingered shirts at thrift stores. While on the bus. At the park. The grocery store. The gym. The moment he left the rental property, the question buzzed. Bryce had tried to get him involved in projects, even modeling gigs—*you've got that brooding, Byronic thing going*—but Ezra hadn't ever wanted to be in front of a camera, only behind one.

"That's smart," Hudson said. "It's a terrible racket."

Ezra wondered if he meant it. There were rumors that Hudson might be inching his way into politics. He didn't seem bothered by it at the moment—hands loose in the pockets of his shorts, strolling as if he hadn't a care.

"I see you taking pictures out here some evenings," Hudson said.

A red-and-green hummingbird zipped by, as if on cue. Ezra didn't reply at first, because he couldn't guess what Hudson was getting at, and there wasn't really any question for him to answer. Was he worried Ezra was paparazzi? "I'm only a nature photographer."

"Not human."

Ezra hazarded a quick laugh. "Right." He kind of wished he hadn't lied, but felt the need to say something definite.

Hudson frowned, eyebrows mossy. He clasped his hands behind his back, accentuating his paunch, and peered at him from the side. "May I see some of your photos?"

"Yeah. Sure. Should I bring them out?"

Hudson glanced back up to the mansion. "Would you mind if we went to the pool house instead? It's unbearably hot."

A car alarm went off in the distance, followed by the quack of it switching off.

"Okay," Ezra said.

They started down the lawn. Hudson wanted to see his pictures? In the pool house? Ezra began to feel a distance from his body, which felt almost like indifference, though he knew from experience that it was stress to such a degree that his body couldn't handle it. Probably later, when he was least expecting it, the panic would arrive and he'd feel a compressed version of everything he hadn't felt at the time.

Hudson cleared his throat and shot a wad of spit across the lawn.

A new thought occurred to Ezra—an unlikely one, but still plausible: the photos *might* make an impression. Perhaps Hudson was a photography aficionado. Who knew? Maybe he'd planned to cover the walls of the mansion with nature photos. Or perhaps he was a patron. He'd heard rumors of closet altruists who enjoyed having clusters of artists they supported, people kept vaguely in their employment whose projects they could talk about with other wealthy friends over hundred-dollar bottles of wine and incredible cheese.

Ezra'd be happy to be a topic of conversation. Maybe he'd get a chance to pitch his dream of photographing birds of paradise in the rainforests of the South Pacific. He figured it'd be nothing for Hudson to secure a gallery opening downtown, much less a private chat with magazine editors.

They arrived. Ezra opened the door and realized that he hadn't cleaned, plus he'd left an adult magazine on the couch. He nabbed it. "I apologize—"

Hudson waved away the concern and took the magazine from his hands. "We're men." He thumbed through the magazine, spread the centerfold, and shook his head. "Weak issue. The girls almost look CG. Over the last few months, it seems they're trying to convince us of a shortage of beauty in the world."

Ezra contrived a laugh. "How about a drink?"

Hudson flipped through a few more pages. "A beer if you've got it."

Ezra grabbed an IPA from the fridge and key-chained the top. They were silent again, and it occurred to Ezra how much people would pay for just five minutes to pitch to this guy. What the hell did he want?

Hudson set down the magazine, took a swig of beer, and paused in front of one of the photos on the wall, a close-up of a male Costa's hummingbird, shiny purple gorget reaching down its chest. It had received third place in a contest put on by one of the second-tier nature magazines. "Amazing how much effort they put into keeping still."

"I took that photo by the bed of foxglove and hyssop in the northwest corner," Ezra said. Over the last few years he'd slowly populated the garden with dozens of species of flora—aloe, beardtongue, bottlebrush, trumpetbush—to attract hummingbirds so he could photograph them. Considering the water shortage, the grounds were still immaculate. He couldn't stand them to be otherwise.

"Here?" asked Hudson, pointing at the floor.

"Yes, sir."

Hudson toasted Ezra with the beer.

"I'll bring out a few more pics." He left Hudson with the photographs on the wall. From a drawer in the living room desk he slid a manila envelope containing his best shots, a portfolio he'd been hoping to someday release as a book. He tried to steady his hands while giving it over.

Hudson sat down on the couch and crossed one leg over his knee and set his beer on the side table. He unfolded a pair of glasses from his breast pocket, leaned back, and began looking through the photos, occasionally licking his finger and thumb in order to separate the prints. He said nothing, only grunted occasionally, mouth slightly open.

This was hell, witnessing someone examining your art. Ezra excused himself, claiming he needed to use the john, and instead walked down the hallway to his bedroom. He sat down at his desk and flipped open his laptop. He scrolled through all the hummingbird photos Hudson was at that very moment judging, and felt his shoulders tighten as each bright image filled the screen. All the potential flaws in the photographs glared back, and for a moment he wished he'd touched them up. But weren't the imperfections what made them more realistic? Didn't he prefer it that way?

He couldn't look at these. He closed the laptop and felt his breath shorten. He pressed his fingers into his neck and felt his pulse. Stay cool. Just relax. He glanced at a picture on the desk of his twelve-year-old self and his mother. Her arms were around his shoulders, smile rigged, as was his.

The shot was taken just a few months before his mother's prophesied date of the Apocalypse. By that point in time, a lot of regulars in their community had already dropped out, uncomfortable with the attention beginning to buzz. They were replaced by brand-new believers, many of whom seemed troubled, looking for something, maybe help, maybe a way out, maybe a way to be right. Maybe a more profound way of saying *fuck you* to the world. These new bodies slowly collected until a swarm flew around Ezra and his mother at an ever-increasing speed.

Though he didn't understand it at the time, Ezra recognized now that beneath the forced smile in the photograph, his mother must have felt it all. Every bit of tension, discord, and desperation. She was the Prophetess, the cipher whose words had caused it. Her sensitivity was being tested to its limits. At home, there'd been more and more evenings where she locked his bedroom door from the outside so she could entertain late-night visitors, more subsequent mornings that he had to cover for her at school. As she advised, he would tell them she was in prayer, which—granted—she most likely was: when he'd leave for school in the morning after one of her bad nights, she'd often be on her knees by the couch, eyes closed but surely bloodshot, hands clasped, muttering.

There was one evening during that time when Ezra was awakened from a light sleep by his mother's drunk, thick-tongued voice calling out. He jumped from his bed and opened the door—surprised it wasn't locked—and ran from his room. He never outright worried that something terrible might happen during one of her fits, but neither did he sleep well.

She was sitting cross-legged on the floor, in her bathrobe, the knobs of her knees jutting out, both scaled and bruised a purplish red from so many years spent in prayer. A late-night talk show gleamed in the background. She stared blankly at the screen, her eyeliner streaked and blotched, though she wasn't crying anymore. Suddenly her face contorted and she again hollered his name.

He grasped her shoulder. "Mom."

She looked up, startled.

He pulled back his hand. "It's me. Ezra. Are you okay?"

Her eyes bore into his. There was recognition in them, but also distance. "There's something you need to know."

"Mom, it's really late." He held out a hand. "Let me help you to bed."

She took it and pulled him down so they were sitting side by side in front of the television. "It was a Saturday," she said. "Fourteen years ago." She continued the story as if in a trance:

she was at church late, alone, preparing nativity cutouts for the Sunday school class the next morning, part of her job as the youth minister. She was single, but had many suitors; in fact, one earnest parishioner had asked her to marry him just the week before. But she'd declined. She'd decided not just to save herself for marriage, but forever. She would be married to the will of the Lord. This wasn't something she'd told anyone, because she was still afraid of what people would think, and she had yet to come to terms with her gift of foresight. There in her tidy office she finished the last of the paper lambs before gathering her purse and flipping off the lights.

She closed the door to the church, the snow light and twinkling and unprovoked by wind. The parking lot was empty, save her sedan and a white pickup truck parked a few spaces away. The church itself was tucked back from the main road, crowning the middle of a large field guarded by tall hickories. The sun had long since set, but the coating of snow reflected the smallest bit of porch light. Ezra's mother paused at the steps and that's when she saw the pickup truck.

"I thought maybe someone needed a safe place to spend the night. Maybe they'd been evicted from their home," she told Ezra, and laughed, scratching her elbow.

She continued, saying that she'd liked to think that her church would be such a place where one would seek refuge. So she held the chilly rails and made her way down the icy steps. The frosty, sucking sound of the truck door opening made her stop for a moment. Someone with broad shoulders slid out of the cab. She could see the orange dot of a cigarette swell and then taper, but she could see little else. The shadow began walking toward her, arms slumped inward as if its hands were in the front pockets of its pants.

"Hello," she called out.

The shadow didn't answer. It kept walking toward her, and once again the little bloom on the end of the cigarette glowed and vanished, leaving a trail of smoke behind.

"Stop," Ezra said to his mother.

She kept talking.

"Please, stop." Ezra turned and tried to run away but she grabbed him and held him there and made him listen. "No. Please."

But she kept going. What he would have given to break into her memory and tear that man from his mother and pummel him until he could no longer lift his arms.

Then, not realizing what he'd done until he'd already done it, Ezra broke away and slapped her. He couldn't forget the awful sound, there in the room, just the two of them, so terrible and intimate.

She blinked. "You need to hear this, Ezra. What you just did is proof. The sins of the father are visited on the son for generations. You need to feel this so that it won't be true for you."

He couldn't look at her. He felt marked by what he'd done, by what his father had done. It was already festering inside him.

"Look at me," she said.

He wouldn't.

"Look at me, Ezra."

He looked up at her, crying and wanting to die.

"I have you because of this."

"He—"

"Was a terribly broken man. But look at what came from it. Look." He glanced up. She was pointing at him.

"I—" he started, but couldn't put words to what he felt.

"You are my son. *My* son." She reached out and grabbed both of his hands. "The Lord turns everything to His will."

Hudson grunted loudly from the living room and Ezra woke from the memory. His toes felt bright with static. He forked his fingers through his hair, took a deep breath, and flipped the picture facedown.

"Ezra?"

He hurried into the living room. Hudson's arm was stretched out along the back of the couch. The television was on, photos back in the envelope. Hudson muted the sound and looked at Ezra. "You look pale."

"It's nothing," Ezra said. He could feel sweat beading on his brow. "A yellow jacket got in the house." He rubbed his elbow as if stung.

Hudson studied him. "Sorry to hear it." He tapped the envelope of photos lying on the couch. "I like your photos."

Ezra tried to gather some poise. "Glad to hear it."

"I fear my wife is sleeping with other men."

Ezra stopped.

"For all I know she's slept with you. You're an attractive guy." He uncrossed his legs and stared. "Remarkably so."

"No," he said. "No, sir, nothing . . ."

"I'm kidding. You would have been a lot more nervous if she had. I can tell when people are trying to hide something. No, you're just nervous because you're wondering what on earth I want. And I saw your magazine—Sybil was in last February's issue."

Her image, laid out on cream satin sheets, flashed in Ezra's mind. He opened his mouth to speak, but what could he say? All Hudson needed to do was ask to see his camera, turn it on, and scroll through the pictures he'd taken the night before.

"—and you're trying to shift the blame to some bee."

"Mr. Hudson—"

"Now don't worry. Half of the people in America have seen her naked. I don't care about that. I just don't want them fucking her." He laughed and gestured for Ezra to take a seat.

Ezra complied. His throat felt parched. He couldn't find a place to rest his hands.

Hudson leaned forward. His reading glasses edged to the tip of his nose. "You're already taking bird pictures in the yard, so this should be simple. What I want is for you to take pictures of any cars that drive up—license plates would be ideal—and of any men you see hanging around, etcetera, etcetera."

"I—"

"You'll never have to sneak around inside the house or do anything illegal. Just be around. Hell, you already are. For all I know you have pictures already. Do you? No, don't answer that. Unless they're with other men."

Hudson appraised him. Ezra'd never seen that look in a person before, both cold and savage.

But then, as if it were nothing, Hudson's glare vanished, and his warmth returned. He patted his thighs and got up. "No matter. What you need to know is that, from here on out, I will match whatever you get paid now for the garden, even if you don't find anything."

"Mr. Hudson, I don't know."

"I'm returning to Vancouver for a few weeks. I just want you to think about it. No, that's not true. I want you to do it. You won't be out of a job or anything if you decide against it. I don't like to manipulate the people who work for me. This is just an opportunity to make a little extra on the side. When you think about it, think about the money. Don't think about my wife or our relationship. That isn't your concern."

His concern? That was the least of them.

Hudson chugged the last bit of beer and handed over the empty bottle. "Thanks for the drink," he said, walking toward the door. "When I get back, I will be prepared to write you a check." He stopped beneath the awning and turned. "Hey."

"Yeah?" Ezra stuffed his hands in his pockets before he could realize how much the gesture revealed.

"I know that I can be a little, well, intense. People around me are used to me being brash. They learn not to take it personally. But we've never met, so there's no way you'd know that."

Ezra nodded.

"You've got to understand, Ezra, that she's my wife. I love her."

"Of course."

"And for that reason, also, you must realize that no one can know about this." Hudson slapped Ezra's shoulder and gripped it. "Good man." He turned and left.

Ezra crept to the window and watched as Hudson hiked up the lawn. As much as the setup and content of the conversation bothered him, the last bit pleased him in a fundamental way he didn't like, nor understand. Was it that he felt included? Flattered? Was it being confided in by a great man, or as simple as being in his presence?

Or was it that Hudson's tenor and confidence reminded him of his mother? Dishing out advice to congregants, slamming down a take-home point on the Sunday morning pulpit, then afterward standing by the front steps glad-handing in that warm, inviting way ministers often have. Ezra knew that—Hudson being a tenant—his attention had already, in a way, been bought. While Hudson wasn't selling something like discipline or virtue, he did want Ezra's trust. And it didn't take a pastor's kid to know how thin the line was between trust and obedience.

Ezra watched until Hudson disappeared into the mansion. He felt ashamed that being told what to do comforted him. Who, deep down, didn't want a patriarch or matriarch? Someone with power to look over your interests, guide you toward your next move? He wasn't proud of it, but it was one of the things he missed most about his mother: to have so many decisions already made, so many questions already answered, so many thoughts already, well, thought. People spoke of deference as though it wasn't among the greatest temptations a person could face.

He sat down on the couch and picked up his portfolio and flipped through the photographs. They were beautiful, damn it. He wished he could claim that mattered more.

FOUR

That night, in the back booth of a diner, surrounded by signed black-and-white photographs of movie stars and ballplayers and various other items of paraphernalia meant to make a person nostalgic for a time they never lived, Ezra sat with his two best friends, Bryce and Maria, who'd been together for just over a year. They'd parlayed their weekly get-together into a birthday party for Ezra. The overhead speakers warbled Elvis and everywhere wafted the smell of butter and sugared rolls and all the foods Ezra never allowed himself to eat.

He finished telling his friends about the recent developments with Sybil and Grant.

"Bro. Bro," said Bryce. "It's just like the movies. Pool boy handed the forbidden fruit. Here's what you do: Take his money *and* get with Sybil Harper." He smirked and tugged at the neck of his black Milky Way T-shirt, which was half-covered by a green flannel with cuffs flipped back at his wrists. A personal trainer, he was tall, broad, and cut like a linebacker. After a decade of auditions, Bryce's dreams of movie stardom tempered into hopes of landing a recurring role on a sitcom, or perhaps a string of commercials. Then he could quit his job and fully commit to his high-concept screenplay, which involved space, time travel, and heroic deeds. "After that? Sell the pictures."

Maria shook her head and looked to Ezra. "That must have been tough. I mean, feeling that Grant Hudson might be into your photos." She searched his face, probably for any sign of hurt. She was a physician's assistant and had come straight from work, wearing scrubs dotted with colorful, nondescript birds. As far as Ezra knew, Maria had no industry dreams. But a few years back she'd lucked into a spot for a big pizza commercial, posing as an everyday customer, which ended up paying for an industry card and a couple of years of grad school. "And Sybil Harper putting you in a bind . . ."

"I hear she likes it that way," said Bryce.

"It's no big deal," Ezra replied to Maria.

She was earnest without fail, and in that way the opposite of Bryce. The two of them lived together and slept together and were married in most everything except name. Ezra considered her the perfect woman. Smart, sweet, independent, and with no edge. Not that she was dull; she just didn't seem to feel the need to impress or top anyone, which itself was intimidating. He admired her. Looked up to her. Could have loved her, even, but there was a problem, beyond the fact that she and Bryce were together. He didn't yearn for Maria in the gloomy way he did for other women. There was a darkness missing. A desperation. Ever since his mother had passed—no, even before that—Ezra's deepest arousal came from tragedy, which was one of the many reasons he never allowed himself to pursue anyone, nor surrender to anyone's pursuit of him.

Bryce started talking about some new brand of organic greens he'd purchased for his iguana. Ezra took a small sip of beer, rubbed his thumb into the tabletop, and considered both of their reactions to Hudson's proposal. How the two of them hadn't considered, other than as a joke, that he'd do what Hudson asked. Talk about having no edge: he, in their eyes, was the epitome of dull, virtuous consistency. They assumed the money and sex weren't even a temptation.

That they hardly knew him was Ezra's own fault. For years he'd presented himself as being as neat and tidy as the grounds he kept. Which wasn't to say there weren't benefits to the act. Bryce and Maria respected him, trusted him, and liked having him around. And though he felt bad about it, fooling them at times made him feel superior—and that feeling in his life had been rare enough to covet. He suspected it was the same feeling that had sustained his mother for years—that delicious knowledge of being sly, enigmatic. He remembered her saying one night, near the end, *God's power rests not in our certainty, but in our doubt.*

But what was the cost of evasion? Loneliness. And after a while, loneliness wasn't situational but organic. A habit. An approach. With most diseases you could question how much control it had versus its host, since they were at odds. In this kind of loneliness the two worked together. Ezra felt both manipulative and wooden, as if he was his own marionette.

This feeling wasn't new. As Bryce and Maria sipped their drinks and used the argument over his situation as an avenue to flirt each other into foreplay, Ezra's mind veered toward a moment where he felt a similar woodenness—a time he wished he could forget.

He was nine, maybe ten, in the gymnasium of the small school run by his mother's church. Metal cages encompassed

clocks and dome lights dangled from the ceiling. One of the
teachers struggled through a ragtime hymn on a pitchy upright
piano while students milled about, most crowded in front of the
industrial-strength fans posted in the four corners of the bas-
ketball court, yelling at each other over the hum. It was nearly
summer and the air was virile with sweat, as was Ezra's body—
particularly his legs—which stuck to the hardwood floor as he
waited for the weekly assembly to begin.

There was a trace of fresh pine wax in the air, but the stench
of bird shit overpowered most everything else. In congruence
with the theology of the Prophetess, Ezra's school hosted a
plethora of colorful, omnipresent birds. They fluttered. Preened.
Pecked seed from the massive feeders hanging in every corner.
Roamed freely through every classroom in the school, every
hallway. This was not strange to Ezra. It was the part he loved
the most growing up. It was home.

A school bell rang bright through the chatter. The piano
music stopped and one of the teachers began a slow rhythmic
clap as other staff members unplugged the fans. Soon the students joined in and clapped in rhythm, faster and faster, until
a teacher up front gave a quick flick of the wrist and everyone
went silent.

A thin, pale visitor with a short beard and wavy brown hair
strung into a ponytail skulked up to the foldout stage. His loafers, jeans, and T-shirt were black.

"Who's this weirdo?" whispered a girl seated in front of
Ezra to her friend.

Despite himself, Ezra wondered how the visitor onstage
would look naked, if his penis would be just as skinny and pale
as the rest of him, if his hair below would be just as dark as his

beard and eyebrows. In an attempt to shun that image from his head, Ezra pinched the skin on his forearm, which was already dotted with bruises.

"I understand that you've heard," the visitor said, speaking as if every syllable deserved its own consideration, "of God's anger over our sinful and degenerate culture—"

As the visitor held forth on the many varieties of sexual sin, Ezra scanned the room in search of relief from his guilt and the arousal the sermon was causing. He browsed his way to the back and caught his mother's glare. She stood in a magenta suit, arms crossed, black hair perfectly parted and falling in equal shares down her shoulders. She flared her eyes at him and tilted her head toward the stage.

Ezra turned back around.

"—Do you know why I haven't allowed myself to see the sun for the last two years?" The visitor put his hands near his crotch. "Do you want to know why I wake up every morning and wrap my privates in copper wire?"

There was murmuring. The two girls seated in front of him snickered and leaned into each other to whisper. Ezra imagined his own penis, wrapped in cold metal. The thought aroused him further. He pinched the skin of his arm and twisted until pain overtook the pleasure.

From the piano in the corner came an awkward, tinkling hymn. From the back row, the rusty wheels of a cart began to screech, announcing the procession of large goblets of honey mead and small bowls of mustard seed.

"I can feel it from up here: your guilt, your shame," the visitor said, roaming the stage. "I'm talking about sacrificing those evil desires brewing in your heart. Give them over!"

The pitchy piano music swelled, and with it, Ezra's body and nerves.

"He's actually pretty good," whispered one of the girls seated in front of Ezra.

"Anointed," said the girl next to her, absently. But Ezra could have sworn there was a gloss to the second girl's eyes, and a gathering of small dark smudges on her forearm . . . were those bruises? She glanced back at Ezra and placed her palm over her forearm and, after a brief look of terror, said, "All these little perverts need to hear this."

Ezra said, "Amen," and busied himself in retying his shoes.

A pigeon hiding behind one of the lamps flew up into the rafters, startled. The visitor froze, as if in a trance, hands out, fingers curled. His eyeballs rolled back and his mouth fell ajar, eyelashes fluttering. The piano player stopped and everyone hushed and waited.

The visitor took a deep breath, clasped his hands together, and continued. "The Lord has just given me a word for you. Did you know that every thought you think is as good as a deed, if not worse, for its secrecy?" He looked right at Ezra.

The tinkling on the piano commenced, then louder, rousing.

"Now," the visitor said, pointing to the ground, "before you even dare step up here and partake, I want you to make a commitment. Among your friends and teachers, among the great cloud of witnesses in heaven. Who of you little devils wants to get serious about your private evil?"

Ezra looked around, stomach clenched, sweating. A few young kids raised their hands as if wanting to be picked for a kickball team. A handful of others did as well, looking bored.

But then his fifth-grade teacher, a busty, hawk-nosed woman whose beauty had compelled Ezra to pinch more than a few bruises on his arms, hurdled around kids and up the walkway from the back of the gymnasium to stand first in line to take the elements. She turned on her heels to the rest of the audience, eyes glimmering with tears.

Ezra tried to adjust himself in his seat but found no relief. His taut little organ rebelled by pressing further into the tight area between his thigh and the fabric of his underpants and shorts.

"See, your teacher is giving herself over. She wants the peace!"

The teacher fell to her knees, her cheeks and neck blotchy and irritated. She grabbed handfuls of the hems of her skirt, revealing her skinned knees. Ezra buckled over as waves of pure, unbridled pleasure soaked through him. When the orgasm slowed, he looked back up to see the speaker's finger pointed directly at him.

"Do you see the struggle of your classmate? The devil inside him, fighting?"

Ezra shivered with pleasure and embarrassment and looked down. The navy blue of his shorts began to darken. The sound of the preacher's voice, the piano, and the shuffling of his fellow students around him faded. *I am a piece of shit,* he thought.

When he opened his eyes, everyone else was standing around him, watching as he kneeled. The piano went quiet. There wasn't a sound. He could see it in their eyes—most assumed he was on his knees praying, experiencing some sort of holy moment that they were not. Even the girls in front of him gazed in wonder.

That they thought he'd experienced some sort of epiphany with the Lord? It was something. It may not have been the truth and the light, but it was a way.

"Have you received a message for us, son?" the visitor asked from the stage.

What else could he do, but pretend? Mimicking the preacher, he held out his arms in front of him, fingers curled, and let his jaw gape. He rolled his eyes back in his head, fluttered his eyelashes, and stopped. It was completely silent. He took a deep breath and raised his hand and pointed to the ceiling, to the birds, to the sky, and to the heavens.

Yes. He was his own marionette. Except for that one part he couldn't bury.

Don't listen to her," said Bryce. "Bro, this is jackpot. It's all under the table. Hudson can't get at you. And dude, Sybil Harper?"

Maria scoffed, but Ezra could tell that she loved every dirty word proceeding from Bryce's mouth.

"Sex and money," Ezra said. "What more could you possibly need?"

The waitress breezed by with plates up to her elbows. Ezra glanced up from the table and saw April pushing through the silver rimmed doors of the diner. He hadn't realized she'd been invited. Maria and Bryce had been trying to set Ezra up with her for a couple of months now. Rumor had it April thought he was attractive, or, as Bryce had put it, wanted his *bone*. It wasn't clear if this was true or just his friends' wishful thinking; Maria and Bryce had failed countless times as matchmakers, but they seemed to have endless energy for trying to reproduce in others what they felt for each other.

Not seeing their table yet, April drifted over to the bar and checked her phone while lowering herself onto a barstool. She wore a thin cream blouse and lapis-blue skirt. Classy—sexy even—but she was one of those people who could be stunning in photographs yet off-kilter in person. From Ezra's view from the booth, her shoulders seemed to slouch forward and her back hunched over the bar. She was attractive but skittish, the kind of person who in the old black-and-white movies would be portrayed as having a nervous tic of crossing her arms, looking about, and restlessly flicking ash from her cigarette. She'd worked as a model and had wanted to become an actress, but her allure in photographs didn't translate. As she'd aged, and her soft features sharpened to a more adult ferocity, her modeling career faded. To pick up the slack she found some odd jobs in makeup, which over time grew into a career.

He'd met April a few times and noticed she had a penchant for demeaning others and took pleasure in doing so. It gave Ezra the sense that she was bitter and lonely—though her loneliness lacked conviction. She was still looking for a scapegoat.

Thus, Ezra wanted her. She had dark edges. But it didn't take the gift of prophecy to predict what would happen if they hooked up. He knew he would trade one kind of loneliness for a closer, more destructive one.

Ezra adjusted his camera, which hung from his neck, and snapped a quick picture of her. Maria and Bryce turned. They waved and tried to catch April's attention.

She squinted. Recognition spread to her face.

Ezra stood and pulled out a chair. "They didn't tell me you were coming."

"The shoot ended early." April kissed him on the cheek before giving the same greeting to Bryce and Maria.

The waiter arrived and took orders. When she left, Bryce cupped his hands and whispered loudly to April, "Our little Ezra's in a love triangle."

"Hardly," Ezra said.

"Who's the victim?" April flipped back her hair.

"Who said there was a victim?" Ezra asked.

"There's always a victim," April said.

"Then Ezra," Maria said.

"I vote the other two," said Bryce.

"Who are we talking about?" April asked.

"*The* Sybil Harper and *the* Grant Hudson," Maria said. April smirked.

"Believe it," said Bryce.

"Bullshit."

"Okay," said Ezra. He took a sip of beer and a deep breath. A part of him wanted to provoke April, to stir that darkness they had in common. "It really wasn't that big of a deal. Around midmorning Sybil brought me iced tea–"

"–*vodka* iced tea," Bryce said.

"And then that night she swam some laps."

"Nude," Bryce added. "And might I remind you the pool is right outside where Ezra lives."

"Which is her prerogative," Ezra said. "It's her swimming pool. And she didn't know I was there."

"Oh, she knew." Bryce said. "Dude. C'mon."

"She didn't," Ezra said. "But the interesting part was this: Grant Hudson came by the next day and asked me to spy on her while he was gone, to see if she was cheating."

"Meaning, to take pictures. PI, noir shit," Bryce said.

"Did we really need a clarification?" Maria asked.

"Let's back up," said April, arms crossed. "She was naked?"

"Completely." Bryce rubbed his hands together.

"I think it's really kind of tragic," Maria said. "I mean, she's married."

The waiter interrupted with drinks. Ezra scanned the menu, even though he knew what he wanted, or at least what he was going to order.

April swilled her glass and plunked it down with authority, causing a few lines to spill out and retreat down the bowl. "So Sybil Harper is a slut. I guess it makes sense, considering what I know about her."

In Ezra's mind stirred images of evenings with his mother, her feet up on the recliner, red wine in hand, cigarette between her fingers, talking about the whores of Babylon giving the weather report on the evening news. "Swimming nude in your backyard," Ezra said, "doesn't make you a slut."

"Maybe not. But her film career has set women back a few decades," April said. "Not that that's important or anything."

"Wait. Weren't you once a lingerie model?" Ezra asked.

She stared him down. "Isn't it funny, Maria, how boys find sympathy so easy when it's toward women they want?"

Ezra stared back, thinking of how she had no idea how true that was, but that it didn't mean the sympathy was wrong.

"Just don't get involved with either of them," said Maria. "Do I even need to say that?"

Nobody said anything. Flatware clinked against plates. Ezra watched as Maria flushed and looked into her drink, seemingly embarrassed at the power of her words. Ezra had noticed that people sometimes mistook her gentleness for a lack of resolve.

"Well, since everything is all downer, Maria and I have a fun announcement to make," Bryce said.

"Not now," Maria said, nudging him in the ribs with her elbow. She glanced up at Ezra and for a moment looked as if she had a question for him.

"It turns out we're not just celebrating Ezra's birthday," Bryce said. "I asked Maria to marry me last night."

A grin crept across Maria's face. She dug into her purse and pulled out an engagement ring, then scooted it onto her finger. It had one small diamond in the middle of a band of white gold. She seemed embarrassed, but then blinked her eyelashes and held out her hand, fingers limp, like royalty.

April gasped, got up from her seat, and hugged Maria.

Ezra stood up from his chair and shook Bryce's hand. Then, in a pathetic daze, he executed all of the appropriate congratulations. He wasn't expecting this. No, that wasn't true. Bryce had told him he'd gone ring shopping. But something inside Ezra hadn't let that sink in. He'd never really believed this would happen. Sure, he knew that he himself was incapable of having anything resembling a normal relationship. And yes, they were all good friends, and he wanted the best for them. But it never failed. There was what you thought would happen, and what you hoped in a perfect world might still happen. Hope rarely

Ezra studied all their faces, because he could feel his doubt inside and wanted to be less alone with it. He reminded himself of what he knew about the night his mother woke with the date and time seared into her soul. Had she not run into Ezra's room only moments after it had happened, crazed, fearful, and in grave doubt over what she'd been told? Had she not groaned for days trying to figure out what to do, because who would want such a responsibility?

Had she not performed miracles before, the vision would have been much easier for his mother—and Ezra—to dismiss. But there was the unexplained regression of prostate cancer in an elderly gentleman whose radiation treatments hadn't worked. The bedridden teen whose car accident left her with no feeling below her hips, who proceeded to walk after a simple visitation and prayer from the Prophetess. But most incredible and distressing was her prescient dream.

Years before, she'd awakened with a vision of a scattered pile of bones and a human skull buried a foot beneath the soil, in a gulley among thick fescue and ferns, next to a quick, bright stream. She recognized the spot immediately because she'd hiked past it dozens of times. In the dark of night, while Ezra slept in his room, she hustled to her car and with a flashlight found the spot.

A case that had been cold for nearly thirty years was solved.

But an Apocalyptic prediction was a prophecy of an entirely different scope. The vision tormented Ezra's mother. She didn't want it. She tried to ignore it. But she couldn't, and Ezra alone was with her through it all, afraid, piecing through Scripture and picturing each horrible scene as real. *Real*. A word used called into question the nature of reality itself.

listened to sober logic or sense, never gave a shit about anything so thin as reason.

Ezra sat down and the old springs beneath the vinyl seat covers sunk beneath his frame.

"You guys," said Maria, sliding her hair behind her ears. "You can see this, right? I mean, all of this. It's meant to be."

"I'm beyond happy for you two," April said.

He couldn't look at them. Instead he studied the vintage travel photos trapped beneath the clear plastic table covering. While they celebrated, he tried to smile. Tried to laugh. Tried to encourage. Tried to become that starchy packing material around which everyone at the table could exist, snug. But their joy mocked him. So he did what worked best: retreat behind his camera to record the facts, one click at a time, as the waiter brought desserts, as Bryce and Maria whispered sweet nothings to each other.

April stared at them. He wondered if she was jealous too. But then she sighed and turned to him, cheek resting on her fist. "So," she said. "Tell me more about your photography."

He cleared his throat and hoped his voice would hold. "I'm most interested in birds," he said. "Hummingbirds in particular . . ." He drew out his answer, reveling in the safety of explaining a solitary hobby that could in no way be offensive to anyone, ever. He didn't feel photography was boring, but he tried his best to make it seem that way. His mother would have approved of his misdirection, calling it respect. It felt like building a moat. ". . . it really requires a lot of patience to capture a decent photograph of a hummingbird. I'm up at five most mornings . . ." When he finished with the hummingbirds, he began holding forth on the ever-popular topic of camera features.

Finally, nearly a month after the night of the vision, Ezra's mother broke. For an entire day, she cried. *I have no choice. I have no choice.* Despite all the pain and sorrow and ridicule and lost friends it could cost her, despite all it could cost her son, she would share the news with everyone who would listen, come what may.

It was real.

What she told them was this: *When God promised Abram that his ancestors would number as many as the stars in the sky, what did he ask for in return? A ritual sacrifice. Cut the heifer, goat, and ram in half, he said. But what of the birds? Keep them whole. Keep. Them. Whole. Why, I ask you? They'd be far easier to split than the rest of the animals.*

Her answer was that birds were the closest to a pure spirit inhabiting the earth. *Did the Holy Spirit descend into Christ as a horse? A tree? A butterfly? No. You laugh, but think with me here. You might ask—and you'd be right to, I wish more people would—why, exactly, the Holy Spirit didn't just descend as a human. We're made in the image of God, aren't we? So why didn't God descend as, well, God? And you might also ask why the Holy Spirit needed to descend into Christ at all. Before that point, he was already the Son of God. Sure, the moment was important, a sign for those watching. Sure, John the Baptist needed to perform the baptism to fulfill Isaiah's prophecy. But why, you might ask, a dove?*

The answer had come to the Prophetess in another dream, where she was led by a dove into the eaves of their former church sanctuary a mile away, one they'd acquired from a mainline denomination when that congregation had gone under. *Something was missing from the religion of my youth.*

I didn't know what, but like many of you, I could feel the lack. She found a ladder and scaled the side of the building. Nested just above the old wooden cross were seven mourning doves, all in a row. The smallest of the doves flew over to her and landed on weathered wood, mere inches from her face. It spoke. "Unite with us and what you desire will come to pass."

The unity between birds and humanity has been broken for centuries. Our part is to hasten that reality to prepare for His Second Coming.

And years later, the date had finally come. They were at the beach, waiting for dawn and the arrival of the Four Horsemen. The Atlantic breakers poured in, one after the other, spending the last of their energy in a sandy froth. Overhead, a handful of seagulls negotiated the stiff wind; if not for their subtle adjustments, they'd look suspended. *Purgatorial*, someone joked. A few laughed, but most didn't.

Ezra shivered.

"You're worried," his mother said, tousling his hair. "Me too." She checked her watch. "It's funny how stuff like watches will be worthless from now on. So much is going to change. It's impossible to even conceptualize. We're so stuck in this world." She squeezed his shoulder. "Everything except our soul is made up of everything else."

"What's our soul made of?"

She winked. "We'll find out."

One of the reporters crept through the dune grasses, with a small spiral-topped notepad in his palm. His hair, unmoved by the wind, resembled brown glass. On the outskirts, a photographer in a gray turtleneck snapped pictures.

"I wish you wouldn't make light of this," Ezra's mother hollered to the reporter.

"We have as much a right to be here as you," he said. "And we'll see how this plays out. Do you have anything to share before it happens?"

"Making light," his mother said, ignoring the reporter's lead. "I hadn't thought about that combination of words before. Maybe it will be precisely that."

The reporter smiled and jotted something down. For a moment, Ezra felt like telling him to get out of here, that he wasn't welcome. But he didn't, and not because he felt it would be in the wrong spirit. He feared what the reporter clearly felt—that this was all foolish, just some big mistake—and that doubt shamed Ezra.

"Some space, please," his mother said to the reporter, who backed away and continued taking notes. She then stepped out in front of the crowd, flanked by the dawn. There was less than ten minutes to go. "Now is the time," she yelled, "to confess anything you've been hiding. Soon it will all be out in the open, so here's your chance."

Ezra bowed his head, knowing he'd say nothing, and wondered whether she'd confess all that she did in secret. The man standing next to him grunted. Ezra looked up and saw that he was holding back tears. His wife took up his hand and patted it gently, her eyes still closed in prayer. The man opened his mouth to say something, but stopped.

Someone in the crowd hollered out, "I cheated on my taxes." Ezra looked up.

"Forgiveness is coming," his mother called out. "And to those who don't believe?" She nodded to the reporter and photographer as others came alongside them. "There is still time to repent." She swayed and began to hum.

The previous night, she'd locked Ezra in his room and left the house. He'd heard the door shut and the hum of an engine in the driveway. He tried to rest but couldn't, until around four a.m., when the door to the house finally opened. Her footfalls creaked down the hallway and she unlatched the bedroom door. He'd expected to smell alcohol, to see the pink glaze in her eyes. Her face was puffy from crying; otherwise, she appeared awake and alert.

"Where did you go?"

"I needed to right a few wrongs."

He didn't prod any further. Her appearance revealed the truth of her words. She looked lighter. She'd made her peace with the johns, probably visited each of them and told them the truth about herself, shared with them the gospel as she knew it, and left.

A breeze hustled in from the bay. The rain stopped and the haze of a rainbow appeared out over the remaining mist.

"Speak now," she called out to everyone. "It's nearly time."

There was a buzzing in Ezra's ear. He swatted it only to realize it was coming from inside. He found himself short of breath.

The man next to Ezra coughed and then whispered, "I cheated—" He coughed again and opened his eyes and looked around. "I . . ." he said, blinking. "I cheated on my wife."

Someone gasped. The man's wife turned pale and stumbled for a moment. Ezra stepped out and caught her, but she wasn't having it. She lunged at her husband—who was now on his knees, groveling—and began clobbering him with both fists.

"Forgiveness will come even for those untrue," yelled Ezra's mother. "Confess before time runs out."

The woman stopped pummeling her husband, shoved Ezra aside, and began walking away, back down the path toward the parking area. A few of the parishioners trotted after her, trying to give consolation while still looking back over their shoulder at what was to come.

"Stay the path!" his mother called.

Ezra watched the reporter scribble across his notepad, a grin on his face. The photographer was hovering about, snapping pictures.

"Have faith! There will be no more pain where we are going!"

Ezra looked back at his mother. She was not only undisturbed by what had happened, she seemed buttressed by it. Was she glowing? Her look steeled Ezra.

Precious few seconds remained. He scanned the ocean and something moved through him, like a wave, or a wind. He felt elated. It was wonderful. His doubt had disappeared.

His mother turned and faced the sunrise, hands open in an embrace. Ezra did the same. Orange light streamed out from the edge of the ocean. There was silence. A few people collapsed. But other than that, nothing.

What felt like an hour passed. Everything around Ezra seemed to burst with life. The grasses dancing in the wind, the seagulls in the air, the clouds painted with color—it was all so beautiful.

They waited.

He could hear his heart in his ears, thundering away, and for the first time it seemed miraculous to him that hearts beat on their own, without any permission; all around him hearts were beating in the same way.

They waited.

Life was coursing through it all: worms burrowing in the ground beneath him, spiders awaiting prey just inside the entrance to their nests—millions of them!

They waited.

A mother rested her arm on her daughter's shoulder. Both had their eyes closed in anticipation.

They waited.

Someone said, "Nothing happened."

"Have patience," yelled Ezra's mother, still reaching out toward the sun, which was now a blinding shard just edging over the horizon.

Everyone did wait, for a few more seconds, then more, and more still. But soon it became clear to Ezra that only the common miracles of life and breath and the sun were present, though each felt less miraculous with each passing moment.

"I sold my house and gave the money to charity," someone yelled.

"My marriage is ruined," said the man next to Ezra, still prone on the ground.

Ezra's mother lowered her arms and turned slowly toward them. Ezra couldn't see her face; she was a dark silhouette with the sun bright behind her.

"Hold true," she said. "This is a test. A lesson. Nothing the Lord does is without purpose. We will find meaning in it ere the end."

A lesson. A terrible thought occurred to Ezra. What if he'd somehow prevented the Apocalypse? What if while everyone else had been confessing, out loud for everyone to hear, the Lord had been waiting on him to do the same, and because of Ezra's pride, the Lord had decided to postpone the event? It was absurd, he knew it even as he thought it—who was *he*?—but at the same time, he could imagine how his name would be spoken of were it in Scripture: *All the faithful were ready, but at the last minute the son of the Prophetess proved unfaithful, and for that reason the Lord decided to wait on His followers so that His followers would truly learn to wait on Him.*

A seagull called out. Ezra woke from his daze and realized that the rest of the crowd had dispersed. Only he and his mother were left. He went to her.

She was crying.

"Mom." He grabbed her hand.

"What everyone must think of me," she said.

"I—"

"Ezra, you know. You know more than anyone here. I would never have done this if I didn't—"

"I understand," Ezra said. He really wished he meant it.

"I so hoped it would happen." She wiped her nose with her sleeve. Her hands shook. "It doesn't make sense. We shouldn't be here. We should be with Him."

"I know." He grabbed her hand and squeezed it. He heard a click.

The photographer was kneeling, snapping pictures. Next to him smiled the reporter, hands in his pockets, seeming content to wait for any further developments before going home to draft a column.

Ezra tried to ignore them, but couldn't. "Stop it," he said.

The photographer kept taking pictures.

"Stop it!" he yelled.

"It's fine, Ezra," his mother said. "They have as much a right to be here as we do."

He'd never heard her voice so empty. Ezra realized something far worse about himself than his doubt. Unlike his mother, he wasn't at all sad that they weren't in heaven. In fact, he felt relieved. His only wish, in that moment, was that he was also behind a camera, instead of in front of one.

A cab flashed its brights to see if Ezra needed a ride. He shook his head and kept walking. Maybe, he thought, I should just take the job from Hudson. He didn't like what saying yes made him, but what was he already? The kind of guy who took nude pictures of married women outside his window. The kind who lusted after his best friend's fiancé. Would getting paid for it be any worse? But he knew what was stopping him. It was the same stuff that kept him from letting those shameful moments take over, the same stuff that kept his exploits from being points of pride or indifference. It was why he kept trying to change, or at least pretending he was someone better. Whether he liked it or not, he could never be like Bryce: joyful and shameless. He would never be free. Blame faith, misplaced hope, his mother, father—even stupidity. Regardless, he was tethered.

Footsteps clapped behind him. He turned. April.

"Hey." She stopped to catch her breath. A lowered sedan rumbled by, rattling the storefront windows with bass.

Ezra nodded back in the direction of the diner. "You looked like you were enjoying yourself."

"You're angry," she said.

"I'm just tired. Not thinking straight."

She paused for a moment and folded her arms, as if cold. "I'm sorry if I've done something."

"You haven't. No need to be sorry."

Her fingers played with the latch on her brown leather purse. He nodded that they should keep moving up the street. They could walk for a bit and say their goodbyes. A walk might mitigate her disappointment. And tomorrow was his day off, and if there was ever a night to hit the bottle, this would be the one. It was his birthday. He'd been diligent in his work, so he could sleep in and get back to it the day after.

Next to him, April's heels clacked against a sidewalk grate. They passed by a punk couple wearing spray-painted denim jackets and sporting Mohawks. Their expressions were fierce but they held hands tenderly. He glanced over and noticed the thin strap on April's purse that split her blouse between her small breasts, accentuated by her hands clasped behind her back. He imagined what it would be like to undo the blouse, button by button, and let it fall limp around her body and shoulders. Why couldn't he love this woman? Here she was, beautiful, smart, a friend.

"Someone would be lucky to have you," he said.

She rolled her eyes.

"I'm just saying."

"Then what was all that at the diner?"

"What do you mean?"

"Don't pretend." Her arm brushed his.

"It just didn't feel right. Doesn't feel right. Listen. I'm sorry I've made things weird. You really are great. I mean it. I'm just not at a place where I can take things anywhere." It was true. It had always been true. But this wasn't good: even to be talking about what they could be was intimate. "I'll walk you to your car. And then you can drive me to my car. We don't have to talk. To be honest, I'd rather not."

To be honest, he'd rather duck into one of the empty storefronts and stare into her eyes, run his fingers through her hair, hear her quick breaths through her nose as they kissed.

They jaywalked across the intersection. This block was lined with three-story apartment buildings huddled around pools. The streetlights hummed and bugs zipped around in the glow.

He again felt her presence. The hairs on his arms stood on end, reaching out toward her.

"Listen," she said. "I know you have a thing for Maria."

He stopped. "What? You're kidding." He laughed and continued walking in an attempt to downplay the idea, but felt terror. How on earth did she come to that conclusion? Did Bryce believe it too? Did Maria?

"It's obvious. Don't worry, I mean, she doesn't . . . well, you know Maria. She doesn't pick up on these things."

"That's absurd," he said, about her suspicions. But it occurred to him why it would make perfect sense. April read his disappointment in the diner as him liking Maria. He briefly considered turning around and running back to clear it up.

She stopped in the middle of the sidewalk next to an empty Vietnamese restaurant. "They don't know. And it's okay. I'm not going to tell anyone."

"Honestly. It's really not that." He leaned against the window and felt it give just the slightest bit from the weight of his body. The words were on his lips, the desire to tell her how he really felt. Why wasn't it ever enough to just feel the truth?

"It's just that sometimes when I see people happy . . . I don't know."

He could see in her eyes that this was exactly what she'd wanted, what she'd hoped—his words were an invitation. Maybe he'd misread her. Maybe she didn't really suspect he was into Maria, but had just thrown it out there, because she knew it had to be something—or someone.

She started walking again and he followed.

"I feel a bit of that too," she said, as she pulled the purse strap across her chest with both hands.

He looked away, feeling under attack, just like he had the other night with Sybil outside his window. An empty bus hurtled by.

She stopped at a gray sedan. "My car." He walked around and got in. As she sat down in the driver's seat, her navy-blue skirt tightened. He turned toward the passenger side window so as not to see any more. But he could already feel it roiling inside him. Everything smelled of vanilla and rose.

She turned the ignition. The car hummed to life.

Ezra turned toward her and she kissed him hard and he could taste the sour of wine. His head turned to fluid, his insides swam. God, her soft lips.

He began to pull away, but she'd reached down and unbuckled his belt. He forced his eyes shut and tried to imagine this was someone he didn't know.

She stopped. "What's wrong?"

"I'm sorry. This is overwhelming."

She kissed him hard in response, and he gave in to the desire, the feeling. Oh! Not just to know you're wanted, or to feel that you're wanted, but to experience it. He felt her blouse

slipping from her shoulders, and it wasn't anything like anything he could compare it to—it provided a new definition, the
slick, watery feel of her clothes being shed like some sort of
skin between his fingers, the buzzing in his chest, the soft, warm
feel of her skin to his touch, the encouragement of her tongue
spelling words of desire in his mouth, and on his cheek, on his
neck, and down.

He knew a better man would have stopped this, would have
said no out of respect and duty, so as to not lead anyone on. He
wished he didn't have a choice in the matter, that it was beyond
his control, but he knew exactly what he was doing, and he did
it anyway. When she looked up and for a moment they locked
eyes, he could tell that she mistook his anguish for joy—if there
was indeed a difference.

SIX

Ezra slogged to the kitchen at around seven the next morning and flipped on the coffee maker. His body felt sticky. His eyeballs and sinuses felt dry. His throat had that prickly feeling that often preceded the flu.

April was in the other room, still asleep on her back, mouth propped open to reveal a transparent retainer covering her top row of teeth, through which her breath every few moments whistled, but that wasn't what had kept him awake through most of the night. After an inelegant, grunting intercourse—an exercise that took ten minutes, total—she'd popped in the night guard and fallen asleep, leaving him to toggle for most of the night between varying degrees of arousal, fear, and shame. And the times when his nerves weren't partaking in that unholy trinity, they'd relax into a deep melancholy over Maria and Bryce's upcoming union.

At three a.m., during one of those drowsy fits, he'd dreamt he was standing up front at their wedding ceremony when lush locks of thick-bladed grass began growing from every pore on his body. He floundered and gasped for breath, and when he woke, realized that his sweat-drenched pillow and sheets were spun around him like a cocoon.

The coffeepot beeped. Ezra poured some into a cracked ceramic mug. He looked out the window onto the grounds, and for a moment conjured Sybil Harper in the pool. He muttered to himself as he took a sip. He'd been thirty less than two days and it felt as though already more had happened than in the previous decade. Everything was changing. Maria. Bryce. Their names already sounded like laments. It could never be the same. Unless he coupled with April—and he wouldn't, the previous night had sealed that—his break with Maria and Bryce would be like a zipper slowly tearing apart at the teeth. Soon they would develop a new group of like-minded couples. They'd try to keep him involved, but then they would get pregnant, or adopt, and at most he'd get a great relationship with their kids, his role becoming that of a babysitter so they could go out and have fun without him.

Ezra sipped some hot coffee. It turned his tongue to cake. He walked back to the dim bedroom and stood above April. She lay spread-eagle in bed, covered by a sheet, flannel blankets flung to the floor. There was no show here, no posturing, and he found himself more aroused because of it.

Memories of the previous night rippled through his mind. Time was already changing them from fumbling intrusions into scenes from a quality porn. April rustled lightly in her sleep and a part of him thought it could work with her. She would never understand him, and he would never be able to be himself around her, but weren't many lifelong partnerships built upon weaker foundations?

But who was he kidding? There was a guy who would charge ahead, and it wasn't him. The truth—he could almost hear his mother's heels clacking across the linoleum—was that he'd taken advantage of April's vulnerability. And now? She wasn't just some code on a screen blipped from existence with a click of the mouse.

Ezra picked up his camera from the nightstand, snapped a picture, and walked through the house to outside. Morning mist dampened the air. He took a deep breath that still felt too shallow. The dim sunlight let his eyes relax. He focused on the lawn, cool beneath his bare feet. He tried to care about his red Marvels of Peru, whose tubular blossoms only puckered before the onset of the midday heat. He wondered for a moment what Hudson was doing in Vancouver, whether he was at that moment behind a camera as well. Whether he expected Ezra to find anything.

He sat down a few yards away from the blossoms, back to a palm, camera in one hand, coffee in the other, and tried not to think. A hummingbird helicoptered toward the grove of Marvels. Ezra struggled to lock it into his viewfinder. It had the signature iridescent gorget surrounding its face and neck, changing colors with every sharp move. What a gift, to be able to truly present yourself in whatever light you wished. Another hummingbird flew into sight, this one flashing a turquoise gorget covering nearly its entire breast. It zipped to a flower and stuck its head inside the lobes. He imagined its slick tongue lapping through its long beak into the chalice.

Then a chill rushed through him. A panic attack. Could he get a break? His heart galloped and his throat clenched. His fingers tingled and then his hands, and he quit breathing through his nose and began to pant. Here it was, the thunder following the lightning of the previous night. As always, waiting for the most peaceful time to boom.

The door to the pool house opened behind him. He pretended to take photographs while listening to April's flip-flops thwack against her heels. She stopped just behind him. Through the corner of his eye he saw the faint etchings of her shadow.

"I'm surprised you're up," she said.

He kept half his face snug behind the camera. "Me too." He heard her yawn and imagined her lithe body stretching. "There's coffee inside."

"Already got it." She sat down just behind him.

A small female hummingbird sparked into view, colored beige and gray with a few white specs and a glossy, understated pink breast patch. Ezra tried to zoom in close but he kept missing the angle or losing sight of it altogether. Pretending to care about taking photographs was much more difficult than caring about taking photographs. His hands shook with yesterday's nerves. The hummingbird darted up to a cluster of red blooms, hovered, then zipped out of the yard just as the sun crested over the hedge bordering the pool house. He set down the camera in the grass.

April was in a bathing suit, a simple yellow two-piece. She must have had one stashed in her car, with her mouth guard, and—now that he thought about it—probably ample supplies just in case of an earthquake, if not a week in Cabo. She sat Buddha-style, towel beneath her, mug of coffee still steaming in her palms. Her olive skin looked soft in the dawning sun.

"Taking a swim?" he asked. A little quaver from the panic attack affected his voice.

"You're shivering. Are you cold?"

"No. It's fine. Just a little amped on coffee."

"I can get you a coat," she said.

"I'm fine." He fidgeted with the camera. Her comment frustrated him more than it should have. It was a small knockoff of what his mother would do: never listen, come to a conclusion about how things were with him and push until he gave in.

But no—as he watched her—there was another reason he resented April, far stronger than any comparison: she was gorgeous. God, there was a power to a beautiful woman that mocked all reason, a power far greater than anything based on hard work or achievement. Anyone who said otherwise was lying to themselves. All throughout history, musicians wrote songs, poets wrote verse, businesspeople made money, politicians grabbed power, and generals launched thousands of ships, willing to kill and sack and pillage and burn, willing to sacrifice the lives of those in their stead, the lives of their loved ones, even their own lives—yes, the world was built and the world burned because *damn that woman was beautiful*.

April took a sip of coffee and stood up. As she walked over to the pool she passed her hand behind her bottom in what seemed like a subconscious attempt to hide it. She slid in and dunked. Then she lay back and began floating, her legs and arms strumming the water.

Have mercy. He began removing his shirt to get in with her, but stopped: it felt like he was being watched. He glanced toward the mansion and there stood Sybil in that huge window on the third floor, wearing a bright purple robe.

"What's up?" April asked.

"My boss." Now he did, in fact, feel cold.

Sybil vanished from the window.

April remained standing in the pool, the failed arch of her back making her look both noble and tragic. "Is it okay that I'm in here?"

"Yeah." He turned back to the mansion. "As long as they aren't using it."

April smirked. "Think she's jealous?"

He turned and winked at her, something he'd never done before—a wink?—but it felt like the best way to be nice. She was fishing for compliments, not that he could blame her.

The door to the patio slid open. Sybil strolled into the courtyard holding a flute of something green. She drew closer and lifted the rim to her mouth, then wiped her lips with her fingers. "Am I interrupting?" She spoke only to Ezra while nodding to April in the pool.

Her voice was familiar, and it wasn't. Not as clear and strong as when he'd heard it in movies, but soft, gentle even. "Not at all," he said.

"I can get out," April said.

"No worries," Sybil said. "Mind if I join you?"

The request appeared genuine, as did her smile.

"We'd be honored," Ezra said, and immediately regretted how stupid that sounded. He didn't know exactly how to do this. Nor did he know what this was.

"Honored," Sybil said. "Well."

Ezra pretended to look around at the yard and at April treading water, but his eyes kept coming back to Sybil.

She began tapping away on her phone. Her blossoming lips mimed the message at hand and she swiped at the screen with her finger. Little lines fanned the corners of her eyes and a few others creased the circles beneath, and in Ezra's eyes she seemed to shrink. She blinked a few times and stuffed the phone into the pocket of her robe.

But then she was back. The confidence. The swagger! Her hands crossed over her waist and loosed the tie around her robe, which opened to reveal a matching two-piece. That sense of watching himself from above returned. She released one arm from her robe before the other so she wouldn't have to set down her flute. It was a small, effortless move, but its elegance was staggering. The robe dropped in a mess on the grass.

From behind, he heard April clear her throat. But he couldn't drag his eyes away from Sybil, who set down here drink and dropped into the pool, feet first, barely making a splash. She rose from the surface and combed back her hair, with her fingernails painted white.

"I'm sorry I didn't introduce myself," she said to April. "You must think I'm rude. I'm Sybil."

"April. You're probably used to people recognizing you."

"You'd be surprised how few do. At least when I have clothes on."

Ezra laughed.

April glided to the side of the pool. "I hear that's rarely an issue."

Sybil glanced over at Ezra and chuckled. "Exactly."

Ezra turned the camera on and off, on and off, the lens spinning. He walked over and perched on one of the recliners.

"Are you paparazzi on the side?" Sybil floated to the edge of the pool.

"Hah," he said. "I'm not. Never." He couldn't tell if she was joking or serious. Did she know about Grant's request? "I photograph hummingbirds. Nature photography."

"Is that what you've been doing? I see you sometimes and it looks from up there like you're taking pictures of the hedges. I thought it was a gardener thing."

"Groundskeeper," said April.

"Ah," said Sybil. "Apologies. Groundskeeper." She grabbed her drink and floated to one of the shallow curved ledges beneath the water and lounged sideways. "I should have asked you guys if you wanted something to drink. Another reason to think I'm rude."

"We had coffee," said April.

"Well, then you're also rude for not offering." Sybil smiled.

No one spoke, though Ezra was trying to think of something, anything to steer the conversation away from whatever this was.

"You know, I worked with your manager the other day," April said.

"Rob?" asked Sybil.

"Yeah, he also works with Coral Massey. I filled in once for her makeup artist."

"I don't know her, really."

"Funny," said April, touching her lip. "She didn't mention that."

Sybil took a sip of her juice and set it back on the ledge. "Well, isn't this pleasant."

"You know," said Ezra. "Before April did makeup, she used to act. And modeled for a handful of clothing companies."

"It's only acting if you get a part. And the modeling was mostly just department stores," said April. "Dresses. Corporate casual."

Ezra noticed that the way she said it was with pride, as if posing for department stores made her one of the people, as if she would have turned down a high-end boutique on principle.

Sybil looked her over. "Yeah, makes sense. You've got the serious professional look going on. You know, back in the day those places wouldn't even return my calls. Probably still wouldn't."

April looked incredulous.

"No, I'm serious. I'm too Hollywood." Sybil dunked her head under the water again, pushed off, and came back up a few feet down the pool. The sun emerged from behind the hedges and its light danced in the water. "That's how it goes. I've carved a niche in the market and now I have to live there." She said it like it was casual, but clearly it wasn't. She drifted slowly back to the shallow end of the pool and reached for her juice.

April looked at Ezra as if to say, *princess*, or something worse.

Sybil put down her glass and exhaled. "Listen to me," she said. "Rich starlet complaining about life. Is that not the height of privilege?"

April shrugged. "Well, yes. It is."

Ezra couldn't believe she said it.

"I mean," April continued, "I know a handful of folks who would be more than willing to trade situations with you, if that's what you're looking for."

Sybil's shoulders rounded off and, for a moment, Ezra could have sworn that her eyes looked larger. But then it was gone and her poise returned. "You know what? Thanks for being honest. Few are, at least not to my face. I'll get your number from Ezra. Maybe when my makeup artist goes on vacation you could do some work for me."

"Gee." April pursed her lips. "That's so nice of you."

"Not an honor?" She looked at Ezra and winked, then lifted herself from the pool, dried off, and let her towel fall in the grass bordering the pool. As Sybil walked back up to the mansion, Ezra managed not to watch. He stared at his feet.

"She's exactly how I thought she'd be," said April.

"How?"

"Total bitch."

"Really? I mean, she seemed a little sarcastic, but—"

"You were too busy gazing at her tits? But yeah, she seemed totally normal."

"You didn't even give her a chance. She was trying to be friendly. She was trying—" He stopped himself, because he knew how it sounded. But he didn't think Sybil had spoken to them like she was some massive star with everything going for her—at first glance, she seemed to feel the same about her life that they did: Dissatisfied. Wanting something else. Wanting more. "She seemed normal."

April scoffed and moved toward the edge of the pool.

"She offered you a job," he said.

"Right. Maybe when my makeup artist goes on vacation you can work for me. Thanks for the scrap."

"What would you want her to do? Offer you full-time work after you called her a spoiled brat?"

"Well, isn't she?" April pulled herself out of the pool and stood. "And, anyways, I would never work for her. Think about it. If she wasn't Grant Hudson's wife, she'd already be out of work. She's a slut, really. A prostitute, with what she does. I could never be a part of that."

"Don't you think that's just a little bit harsh? I mean, wow. How's the view up there?"

She stopped and stared. "Fuck you. You know what? You two are perfect for each other, *pool boy*." She nabbed her towel and dried off. "I can't believe you can't see it. You're straight from central casting. Fucking boilerplate."

"Whatever."

She scoffed and surveyed the mansion, the lawn, the property. "I have no idea why I never asked myself what the hell you were doing here in the first place." Mocking Sybil, she let her towel fall crumpled to the grass before stalking away.

Ezra sat there, dazed. She didn't know a thing about him. This job, this life, it had nothing to do with Sybil. He'd been working and living here for years before she and Hudson ever set foot on the grounds. He stood up from the recliner and sat down at the edge of the pool and dipped his legs into the water. He felt as though he could swim a thousand laps. Behind the pool house, April's car started.

He took a deep breath and looked up at the mansion. He got up and took a picture of the towel that April had left on the grass, then another of the robe and slippers that Sybil had left. Then he took a picture of them both together, as they lay, side by side.

SEVEN

Ezra soaked in the bathtub, a finger from finishing the pint of vodka from the freezer. Even though it was midafternoon, it had seemed like a good idea to drink, because he didn't know what else to do. He ladled a taste on his tongue, sucked it down like an oyster from its shell. He coughed and chuckled. He'd been such a fool, spending years in the delusion that if other people assumed him normal, he'd feel the same way.

He downed the rest of the vodka and remembered an afternoon a few weeks before his mother died. He was thirteen and walking home from school along an alder-lined thoroughfare bordering a street-side creek. A sedan passed by; he recognized one of the kids from school in the passenger seat. He'd been over to their house for dinner once. He knew the name of their dog—Tucker—and that they had to be careful of the big old peach tree in the backyard because bees had built a hive in its upper branches.

The car drove past. No one acknowledged him or offered a ride.

Ezra waved anyway, equal parts the instinctual reaction of his mother's son, performing his duty, as well as to show them he understood what had just happened. As he walked and watched them drive away, he nearly stepped on a small garter snake sunning itself in the road. He started and it slid into the grass and disappeared. He closed his eyes and took a deep breath. He couldn't ignore the truth any longer. Maybe his mother could, now that she'd been put on paid leave by the group of elders who had, up until that morning on the beach, been at her beck and call. Only a handful still believed—like he wanted to—that she'd made a mistake, and that her mistake didn't nullify her prophetic gifting.

They let him stay in the church's K-12, though his class size had diminished by half, and many who were still there wouldn't speak to him. A part of him wished that he could go to school somewhere else, but where would he go? His mother had long been estranged from her own family. When it came down to it, she was all Ezra had. And she was in no place to make any changes, holed up in the living room, barely eating, talking to herself, reading, scribbling manic notes for sermons she could no longer deliver.

Ezra turned down the cul-de-sac and saw his house. One story, white siding with a weathered shingle roof. Mortgage paid by the church. He took a deep breath. Even though school wasn't a joy, it had at least provided a break from home. He walked up the steps and the wood creaked beneath his feet. The door was open. It was shadowy inside. A few finches on the rim of a lampshade chattered. He flipped on the lights and the birds hopped away. He heard a cough from the kitchen. "Mom?"

"Ezra," she said. "Come. I need to show you something."

He set his backpack down on a spot of the couch that wasn't filled with spiral-ringed notebook pages. As he walked toward the kitchen, he noticed that the small cross that had hung above it—as one did in every room in the house—was now turned sidewise. He reached up and righted it.

In the kitchen, his mother was squatting on the floor in a faded blue bathrobe while peering over a photograph torn from a book or magazine. She snapped her fingers. "Come. Come down and look at this."

She smelled of sour milk. As far as he knew, she hadn't showered in a week. It took a few moments to grasp what he was seeing in the photograph. It looked to be a bald man in robes sitting in the middle of a city street. His hands were on his knees, like hers. A few cars were parked nearby. Beyond stood a small crowd of onlookers. It appeared to be a prank. The man sitting in the street was completely engulfed in flames.

"How did he do that?" Ezra asked.

She looked up at him and blinked. "This isn't fake."

It was impossible. The flames seemed to be emanating from him, yet he was sitting indifferently, as though they weren't in fact consuming him. He looked peaceful, meditative.

"It's gotta be a trick."

She took a deep breath through her nose and shook her head. "This generation."

He ignored her insult. Her unwashed hair was stringy and there were a few sores up near her widow's peak. He could feel it on her, a more profound darkness than before. Her pulpit gone and he was now her only audience. This was like one of her difficult nights stretched out over weeks, only she never left.

"I want you to really look," she said.

"I'm looking."

She shook her head.

He tensed up and tried to cork his anger. Was it his fault? Is that what she thought? What had he done wrong? Far less than her. He'd done everything he was supposed to do, at her request. Yet that still wasn't enough.

"Son, move beyond the trivial."

He closed his eyes and took a deep breath. No one else was going to help her, and she wouldn't allow it if they tried.

"A burning man," he said.

"Son, beyond. You are more than that answer."

He studied the man's peaceful face. "A man allowing himself to be burned."

"Allowing," she said. "Yes. Yes." She swiped her hand over the picture and put her hand to her lips. "But it's more than that."

He said nothing.

"Context." She hit her forehead with her palm. "Of course. You know nothing of the context. How would you? I'm sorry. Ezra, honey, this man lit himself on fire and changed the world. Decades later and thousands of miles away, we still can't avoid its symbolic power."

He saw in her eyes what he'd seen many times: a certainty. He felt sick. "There's other ways to change the world."

"People listened. Even governments listened." She closed her eyes and moved her mouth, as if responding to an unknown voice. Then she opened her eyes and scanned his body. "I've always wondered if you would get the gift." She turned over on her back and stretched out on the ground next to the picture, putting her hands over her chest, as if preparing for a burial. "Sometimes I hope you don't. The life of a prophet is one of suffering."

He stood up. She'd talked of suffering many times before, but not like this. "Stop it."

She said nothing.

"Get up," he said, and yanked on her hand. "Do something. You're just sitting here all day every day."

She pulled it away and scowled at him, retreating to her pose. "Your generation wraps themselves in cloak upon cloak. Perhaps it's the only way to get through." She closed her eyes and began humming some tune he didn't recognize.

He stood there for a moment and watched her, feeling angry and afraid. The desire to help her. The desire to escape. The desire to go back in time to when things were smoother. To be part of a family that drove right by when people they knew needed a ride. *It's simple*, he wanted to tell his mother. All of these birds? They weren't anything more than what they'd been created to be. They ate, flew, reproduced, and tried their best to make the most of what they had. They weren't remarkable in the way she thought of them. They couldn't be if they tried. They were just birds. Birds! Her vision was just a dream. Doves were sacrificed whole. Christ was sacrificed whole. The point had been made. Nothing more needed to die that wasn't already dead.

"The dove, mom," Ezra said. "It was a symbol. An important symbol. But nothing more. And that's okay."

She blinked and frowned from there on the floor. Then she stood up, reached out, and brushed the bangs out from his forehead. "You can resist," she said, smiling. "But in the end, it captures you."

"It's not the end." Ezra turned from her and retreated to the cupboards, retrieving the last remnants of an old package of spaghetti noodles for dinner, even though it was only three-thirty.

So often since then, he'd agonized over the question of whether he could have done more. Looking back, with decades of hindsight, he knew he'd had many avenues to help his mom and himself. But he'd been so sheltered, and been taught to distrust those very people whose job it was to help. Did that let him off the hook? Maybe. But it didn't feel like it. Never had.

Back in the pool house, Ezra left the vodka bottle on the soap ledge lining the far end of the tub and got out, drying himself with a damp beach towel while the water funneled down the drain. He pulled on a fresh pair of board shorts, a gray V-neck T-shirt, and covered it with a navy-blue hoodie. He left the bathroom and went to the window overlooking the grounds. The midday sun broke beneath the palms. Ezra rubbed his eyes, forgetting he had contacts in; one popped out, limp and pathetic. He moistened it with his tongue and placed it back on his eyeball, and blinked until the stinging stopped.

He gazed out the window once again. The gray stone mansion seemed unimpressed. He'd probably be better off living in a cave or on the top of some desert spire. He took a deep breath and laughed to himself. What was left? Maria and Bryce were getting married. His tryst with April was an utter failure. And by staying silent there in the pool, he'd all but scorned Sybil.

He imagined this might be how his mother felt while appraising that photo of the burning monk, but immediately felt guilty for how trivial his situation was in comparison to hers, not to mention the monk's. God, to feel so deeply, yet to have those feelings so reasonably dismissed.

It was only a few dozen yards to Sybil's back door. All he needed to do was knock. He'd never be like Bryce, never be what April wanted. He'd never be his mother's saint. He wanted Sybil, every molecule, every atom, and wanted just as dearly the escape her arms provided. Did that make him a monster? So be it.

He opened his door and the smell of chlorine calmed him. He passed the pool and deck furniture and made his way up through the lawn past a crowd of starlings pecking blindly at the parched grass. Above, the thick, papery palm fronds gossiped in the wind. He felt loose, gummy. The Ezra he'd contrived would never have taken such a risk. But what was a risk? Hadn't the last decade without risk been its own quiet catastrophe?

Ezra heard a deep thrush of wind and spotted a large shadow overhead. He turned around. A heron, wings outstretched for balance, landed near the pool and began stalking around the edge, scissored beak and wiry neck ready to spear any fish gurgling up from the chlorine.

Were his mother here beside him, he knew that she'd immediately turn this heron into a metaphor. *Like the heron, you've been looking for a meal where nothing could live. The water appears beautiful, though, doesn't it?* He kept walking. The mansion grew with each step.

"Fuck it," he said. "I'm the most sentimental motherfucker on the entire planet, and I want Sybil Harper." He coughed and wiped his nose. "I want her for her body and looks and nothing else." A lie, but it felt good to say it. A strong breeze picked up and cooled him. He crossed the patio and saw himself reflected as a dark shadow in the checkered windows of the sliding patio door.

Sybil's image appeared next to his and the door slid open. She stood in her two-piece, unconcerned, one hand holding the door handle, the other the top of the awning.

"I don't know what more I need to do," she said.

He took her by the waist. She grabbed a fistful of his T-shirt. He pressed his lips into hers and slid his tongue into her mouth. She tasted of guava. For a passing moment, he thought of Hudson and what would happen if he found out. But she pressed her fingers into his shoulders, and he let his fingers slide down. He closed his eyes as his insides gnashed and sang.

EIGHT

Morning. Sybil slipped from beneath her covers. Wiped sweat from her forehead. Could have sworn her phone was ringing. Over the last few days she'd been hearing phantom calls, both in her dreams and awake. Grant. She was afraid to talk to him, afraid he'd guess what had happened. She really didn't know what he'd do if he found out, what particular form his rage would take, or whether he'd care at all.

She saw a brief glimpse of her body in the full-length mirror as she walked by, enough for a familiar dread to set in. Her beauty was fading, as was her career; matter of fact, they seemed to be competing for which would collapse first. She had a front row seat and no say in the outcome.

Her phone was charging near the sink. She picked it up and checked for any important messages. Nothing. No auditions. No meetings. There'd been times, in the height of her rise, when she would have yearned for a time like this, not realizing that quiet was the sound of a career flatlining.

She let her robe drop outside the open shower. It took her a moment to find the right water temperature. As the stream ran through her hair, she took a few deep breaths and focused on the feel of the air filling and escaping her lungs, trying to be mindful of her body, the touch of the water on her skin, the sense of being *here*: not in the future, not in the past, but in the present, physical world, that balm for a struggling mind.

She'd gone off her meds a week ago, tired of feeling numb. So far, the mindfulness exercises had been enough to temper her nerves. She'd been off them once before, and two weeks in, a bad night visited. She woke, midmorning, on a lawn chair on the patio covered in towels, miserably hungover, having no idea how she'd gotten there—though the towels had to be Ezra's doing, of course, because they were from a hutch near the pool house, and Grant was gone, and none of her people had any reason to visit.

Her people. She chuckled. There were fewer and fewer of those each passing day. More seemed to flee with each emerging wrinkle and cellulite pock.

She hadn't spoken of the blackout to anyone, but took the event as a warning. A reminder that her diagnosis was legit. That modern medicine was legit. She'd once again boarded the SSRI train and chugged along. But the tedium of the passing days and the absence of those bright, wonderful highs and rich, dark lows of a pharmaceutical-free life quickly became its own confinement. Less like a prison than suiting up for a winter snow day, like those she experienced growing up in the Pacific Northwest. Mittens, long johns, puffy bibs, parkas, and all the rest of those layers that her parents threatened her into wearing so that she'd never get to experience how snow felt on bare skin.

She noticed a dark hair on the bar of gritty exfoliate soap. Ezra. He was probably already outside working on the grounds. He was quiet most of the time. Brooding, and in that way, the opposite of Grant. In so many ways, the opposite. Grant's confidence forced itself upon others; Ezra didn't seem to need any more space than what he was given. He seemed grateful, in a word. How the public wanted lovers to appear onscreen. There was a reason for that. It was attractive in a warm way. It felt good to be someone's good fortune.

She finished the shower, toweled off, and took a moment to file her nails over the drain. Someone's fortune: she'd never felt that way with Grant, but then again, feeling that way hadn't been what she'd wanted all those years ago. She'd wanted fame. She and her agent had used words like momentum and trajectory as if a fabulous career was simply a physics problem in need of the right figures. But she'd felt like a pretender, worrying that all of it was just a dream. Delighting in the company of anyone who believed her rise was inevitable.

She combed her hair and her ends kept catching in the teeth. Lately, she wished it all *had* been a dream. That fame hadn't come so quickly, so easily. The whole world was full of Aprils, damning her for voicing even a hint of disappointment. But that didn't change the fact that she hated her situation. Had now for years. Sometimes she wondered if she shouldn't just don a disguise and hop on a plane and never again see anyone from this life.

But she couldn't. She'd only ever gone as far comparing ticket prices to various dreamy isolations. Something kept her from leaving. Something that wasn't small. When she was acting a part, becoming someone else entirely, she felt free in a way that she never could be while being herself. And to know that her fabrications would be seen and judged and valued by those whose opinion she respected? This was no small thing, either.

But that feeling was short-lived, and had become more and more so as time went on. She loathed the way each performance, once complete, was left to be managed by people with grossly different ambitions. She'd watch the films after production and see how much of her pure, initial energy had been left on the cutting room floor, even how a camera angle captured the studio's vision instead of her own. Her parts lost all dimension, ripping the focus from the character she played to her figure and features and however they'd best arouse the audience.

Again she checked her phone for messages. Nothing. She brushed her teeth, inspected blemishes, applied creams, appraised herself, and let the sadness run through her. Only thirty-five, and were it not for those blessed digital touch-ups, out to pasture.

People were wrong, of course: the years didn't take, they traded. Sexual allure for complexity. But who wanted complexity from her? All these films and photo shoots betrayed a bitchy vixen with simplistic desires. And people, all these people, they assumed that her typecast role was a thinly veiled biography. Like that girl April. In her eyes, Sybil was nothing more than a caricature.

Not that she could lay all the blame on others. She knew she was complicit. It wasn't as though she'd put up a fight all those years ago—far from it. She chalked up the attention she received from playing her typecast in real life as proof that she'd finally, at long last, found herself. She was glad to be the vixen. Relieved by it. She was getting everything she wanted. More than she could have hoped and far more than she'd ever experienced just being herself. The phone never stopped ringing. Paparazzi followed her everywhere. And once the Internet started humming in earnest, the melee went to another level. Parties, not-so-secret getaways, rumors, wardrobe malfunctions, vapid heartthrobs, clashes with rivals, trumped-up run-ins with the law—sure, looking back, she could say that it was shallow, that she was click-bait opium, catering to the lowest common denominator, but in the moment, it was her *life*, and life was fucking great, at least while it lasted. Sure, she was off the rails. Self-destructive. Trying to keep at bay the growing fear that she'd long since peaked and the only way to go was down.

Yeah, she was *caught up* in it, but that was no small thing. Anyone who said otherwise was, at best, ignorant. People spent their lives trying to get caught up in something that might make them feel good enough to forget themselves.

People didn't understand what it did to you, being famous. Everyone already knew about you, so they assumed they knew you. All you needed to do was agree, and you could hide in plain sight, and reap the rewards. Yes, notoriety was just another form of anonymity, but what a glorious anonymity could be.

But then a few people tired of you. It started with jokes and unflattering pictures, progressed to caricatures and memes, then everyone started to add *former* to all you'd done. Former B-lister. Former It girl. As in, *formerly* the phone rang. They blamed it on your antics, but it was your face, your name, the sound of your voice. You were no different than a bag of chips displayed by the cash register, binged on one too many times. People knew you by flavor alone, never thinking that you'd been born from an eye, roots stretching out deep into the dark soil, stalks reaching toward the warmth of the sun.

She sat down on the toilet. It was amazing how quickly the drop occurred. She'd fought it, tried to reinvent herself, but only ended up looking more desperate. She enrolled in a poetry class at UCLA, and when word got out, the tabloids mocked her endlessly. She helped build a home for an under-privileged family outside of Oxnard and everyone called her bluff. She went on a medical relief trip in the Amazon and people howled.

She wiped and flushed and washed her hands. God, she needed to stop thinking about it. She closed her eyes, trying to center herself. Breathe. Breathe.

She gave up. In the end it was no use, was it? Trying to pre-vent what had already happened? Trying to forestall the inev-itable? She looked in the mirror and picked at a blemish until it bled. She left the room and circled down the staircase, hand sliding along the reclaimed walnut banister. And so, Ezra, the gorgeous young man whose affection might ruin her further, whose affection she was nonetheless so, so grateful for.

Yes. She needed to stop thinking about everything and everyone and instead focus on this: Ezra would be done work-ing by lunch and they would make love. God it felt good to have a body pressed into hers, to run her hands through some-one's hair without a camera to capture it. Her mind would glint when Ezra buried his lips into her neck. It felt pure, bordering on perfect. Not that it was sterile, or well performed. Thank God it wasn't. He was often awkward, fumbling. Muscular, but not like those gym lurkers whose skin looked like an overripe tomato ready to split. He smelled of soap, but below, faint on his skin, was the scent of fresh-cut grass. And he was less attrac-tive up close. He'd lose the innocence in his face: his thick, dark eyebrows were a mess and his wide eyes and full lips seemed at odds with the rest of him.

But all of that served the wonder. With him, *she* was allowed to be a mess, and pure, and young—and goddamn, how old was thirty-five old? Afterward, they'd relax in bed, sun streaming through the windows, overhead fan spinning. If staged for screen, someone might place a pitcher of ice water with lemon on the nightstand next to the bed and make sure to get a sound bite of ice cracking as it melted.

The balls of her bare feet slapped lightly against the cold shale of the kitchen, numbing the arousal thinking about Ezra had provoked. She knew that from Grant's perspective, she was *using* Ezra. But she'd relied on Grant's perspective for too long, and what had it gotten her? Miserable success.

She caught herself picking at that blemish on her face again and froze. What if she and Ezra were at that very moment being recorded? She glanced around, looking for anything suspicious. The cabinets, the windowpanes, the shelves. She found nothing, of course. And as she considered it, the idea became more and more laughable. This was a rental, and Grant was far too consumed with his own matters to worry about her—that being, of course, the problem, if not the root.

Many times, over the phone, she'd cried about it to her mother, who'd replied—time and time again—*just follow your heart*, until finally, in a moment of frustration, she blurted out *why the hell don't you just leave him*? But her mother's heart hadn't ever desired a career, much less fame and acceptance beyond friends and family. She loved the Pacific Northwest and she only ever wanted to find a good man, raise a family, and live there. And she was there still, to this day, in the Cascade foothills edge at the of the city, only instead of kids to rear, she now had a yard filled with rescue dogs.

Her father's heart might have wanted more: a few times he'd mentioned a mining company headquartered in Juneau and an import/export company in San Diego. But when she'd asked whether he regretted not pursuing them, he'd shifted in his seat and said, with his usual annoying-yet-forgivable condescension, *A better question is whether there are any decisions a person* doesn't *in some way regret.*

In short, her parents' desires never asked them to be anything other than conventional. They were free to judge her ambition and success from the safe confines of their couch without the least worry of consequence.

Like Ezra. How many people would die to be in his shoes— dating a movie star while still living a common life? Reaping the rewards without any of the risk? Didn't they, every night, make love next to a showcase of Grant's awards? Even her bathrobe was embroidered with a *G* looped around her *S.*

Now that she thought about it, *she* might die to be in his shoes.

But here she was, diving into that cycle again. Obsessing over matters that wouldn't be resolved by thinking. She opened the refrigerator and felt the cool air rush against her face. The leftover Brie from the night before made her stomach growl. It would taste amazing in an omelet and the indulgence might bring her back to reality. But she'd crushed her calorie count for the week in the last three days, and she didn't want to get back into the habit of binging and purging. You never knew when a screen test would pop up and she'd be called to take someone's breath away.

A breathtaking role. What she would give for one of those. It had been years. She'd been nominated for one Oscar in that first film with Grant, where she played a prostitute that fell in love with a self-destructive Vietnam vet. As she'd sat through the ceremony, surrounded by fellow actors and industry folks, one of the most profound feelings she'd ever experienced in her entire life struck her dumb. The only way she could describe it was a warm, honeyed glow of belonging. She'd never felt as though she really belonged *anywhere* before that moment.

She grabbed some vegetables and a tub of Greek yogurt and dragged the food processor from the drawer. The blades screamed their way through the hard bits until its contents spun into a tan mulch. Something tickled Sybil's neck and she whipped around, startled. Ezra, trying to kiss her. "What the hell?"

He laughed. "I didn't mean—"

She felt like hitting him. She was amazed at how agitated she'd become just by thinking about Grant and the business. "Aren't you supposed to be mowing my lawn?"

He feigned offense. "*Yours*? It's a rental."

"Go fuck yourself."

He laughed.

She grabbed his arm and pulled him close and kissed him near his ear. He smelled of lavender. He moved to take it further but she pushed him back.

He chuckled and took a seat on a stool near the island.

She poured herself a highball glass of the mush and thought of how easily she'd just slipped back into her role. My God, it frustrated her. As long as she never had to speak with anyone, she could be thoughtful. But the second the outer world intervened, her impulse control went to shit, and she became *that girl*. "I'm sorry," she said. "You surprised me."

"I'm the one who should be sorry." He was wearing a black T-shirt and specks of sweat had soaked through on his chest and armpits. His skin was shining and there were smudges of dirt on his arms.

Just looking at him tamped down some of her anxiety. "No, you're fine. We're still figuring each other out."

"Anything else you want to figure out, before I continue with my duties?" he asked, nabbing a sprig of broccoli from the plate of the previous night's hors d'ouevres.

Anything? He meant sex, of course—the nerd—which, granted, made sense, considering. But if *anything* truly was in play, she'd rather ask him what he thought about the time she'd first met Grant, at that party in some studio head's rental house up north on the beach, and why she'd let that meeting determine the next ten years of her life. She'd come with another actor who knew someone who knew someone and they'd wandered the obsidian floors, trying not to laugh at the ridiculous post-modern trash art vomiting from the walls, and then there was the furniture, which probably cost tens of thousands of dollars but looked as if it'd been cast out into an alley and picked up.

She remembered how, at the party, Grant had grabbed her by the elbow and held her firm, and then looked over her face like he was at the butcher shop inspecting steak cuts for a dinner party.

"Who *are* you?" he'd asked.

"No one," she'd said, because that was precisely how he'd made her feel: no one without his approval, without those impossibly direct eyes carving pounds of flesh from her frame. It was captivating, if to be captivated was a mixture of terror, exhilaration, and submission.

Back in Seattle, at that stupid private liberal arts high school she'd attended in hopes of better pursuing drama, she hadn't even been asked to the lame anti-prom the faculty had organized around their own childhood regrets, even though more than a few of her classmates had likely spent their awkward dates wishing she was on their arm. But Grant? He looked her over and remained unfazed, frosty, emotionless to the point of objectivity. Her entire life she'd been desperate for someone whose opinion wasn't too clouded by relationship or insecurity to tell her who she was.

"You're a star," he'd said, and in many ways, that initial comment—its coldness, conviction, and stern evaluation—held her fast all these years.

So, was there anything she wanted to talk to Ezra about? How about everything, from the very beginning to the end, released slowly into his dark eyes. But there were things she felt comfortable sharing, and things she paid a therapist to listen to, knowing no small part of what she was buying was discretion. "If you really want to know, it's just work," she said. "Looming."

He nodded. "Your next movie?"

"There isn't one, yet. I passed on a dandy last week, about a road trip. It required me to be sexy, stupid, and eventually, dead." She didn't mention the other she'd passed on, which asked that she play the part of the mom who got in a love triangle with her teenage daughter's boyfriend. It was directed by the same guy who'd filmed her most recent picture, which—surprise!—the MPAA had deemed NC-17, but not because the illicit material was artsy. Quite the opposite. She'd agreed to do it out of spite toward everyone and everything during a period of extreme desperation and intoxication. It debuted this last week in movie theaters that catered to perverts and there wasn't a thing she could do about it.

"What sort of role do you want?" Ezra asked.

"I'd take a pizza commercial if the writing was decent."

He laughed and crunched a nub of broccoli, perhaps not realizing that the noise was disgusting. God, he could be such an innocent.

"You really want to know?" she asked.

"Sure." He got up and poured what was left of the shake into a mug.

"How about you show me some of your photographs first?"

"You're into boredom?" he said, taking a sip of the shake. "This is terrible, by the way."

"You're talkative this morning." She gave him a pat on the ass, stepped into sandals, and led him to the entryway.

NINE

They walked out onto the patio and down through the grass toward the pool house. Birds buzzed. The cool morning dew worked its way between her bare toes.

"I'm actually kind of curious to see where you live," Sybil said.

He shrugged, "It's basic."

"Anything's better than that monstrosity." She gestured back to the mansion and felt a kiss of shame. Living there wasn't necessarily better than living in someplace smaller— she'd thought many times she'd be much happier in a cabin in the Alaskan wilderness—but to imply that was poor taste, and murder was easier for the public to forgive than elitism. "I mean, it's fine as far as—"

"—it's okay, I feel you. The outside is foreboding, and the inside—"

"—is nice," she said. "But thanks." They passed the pool. Leaves floated on the water's surface.

He paused. "I'll take care of that later this afternoon."

"No worries," she said. Of course some of his duties had slipped. She'd been the cause. Probably the only reason he'd mentioned it was because she'd tried to take back the mansion comment. By trying to clarify her position she'd only reinforced what didn't need reinforcing. It occurred to her that a part of her feared him, not because he made less money and wasn't famous, but because his position ensured him the public's sympathy.

He laughed, but fumbled the key into the door.

They should have stayed at the mansion. She should have had him bring the pictures up from the pool house. But there it was again; even *up* had its connotations.

Grant was always going on about how equality was child's play, a dream that could only be sustained in a vacuum, because deep down everyone seemed hardwired to enforce ancient social mores. She disagreed on principle, but he had a point. If she wore old sweatpants and a T-shirt to the gym, someone would take a photo that would go viral and she'd be shamed for looking dumpy. Americans claimed they wanted equality, yet insisted on a monarchy, if only to see it suffer.

She reached into her pocket to glance at her messages. Nothing.

When the door to the pool house opened, she was greeted with the smell of Ezra's space, which like him was warm and earthy. The place was okay. She felt a bit guilty for not having known what it looked like. The décor was comfortable: clean tan carpeting, bulbous brown leather couch, a black armchair. The mismatched furniture reminded her of the collection in her parents' basement. The living room opened to a kitchen with new appliances and a decent countertop. On the kitchen table were stacks of magazines, photography and nature. "Your place is nice."

"The neighborhood's decent."

She surveyed the walls and found one filled with photographs, most of which were hummingbirds. A few she recognized were taken on the grounds—she'd spent an occasional boring afternoon, waiting for work, in search of distraction among the flowers. She stopped at a close-up of a hummingbird midflight, its chest splashed with different shades of pink and purple, wet with shine. She enjoyed watching their neurotic flights. "I like this guy."

"Your husband stopped at the same one."

Grant never mentioned that he'd visited. "What'd he want?"

"Do you really want to know?"

The look on his face told her the answer was amusing. "What, did he try to get you to do something for him?"

"How did you guess?"

"That's what he does." If nothing else, Grant had taught her what the smallest of promises—much less, threats—could coax in those with ambition. She continued examining Ezra's photographs, hoping he'd read it as her not caring, hoping he'd just offer up answers on his own.

"He wanted me to spy on you."

"You're kidding." She felt annoyed, but a part of her was comforted. Flattered, even. She couldn't resist asking. "What exactly did he say?"

"He'd seen me taking pictures and asked if I'd photograph any guys who came by while he was gone."

Huh. She was surprised. Not that Grant would do such a thing, but that she'd misread him. Perhaps he didn't assume she was at home, depressed, and lonely. This proved that he at least cared enough to try and stop whatever transgressions her despair might cause. But *cared* might be giving him too much credit. Beneath it all—she reminded herself—Grant was a sad, insecure man, unable to trust, and for that reason, controlling. Case in point: recently he'd been overlooked once again for membership at a country club he'd for years claimed to despise, which of course made him want it all the more. In response, he hired a lawyer on behalf of a disgruntled neighbor of the membership chair so that he might *sue the fucker* for damages caused by a pine tree whose needles had killed the grass of said neighbor's lawn.

"So," she said. "Are you going to take a selfie?"

"It did make me wonder what was up."

"Trust me. You don't want to hear about it." She walked to his kitchen sink and washed what was left of the shake out of her glass. In a way, she felt better: that Grant was asking Ezra to spy was proof that he hadn't set up cameras. "Just so you know," she said, "I've never done this before. There have been no guys coming by the house."

He smirked, hands still stuffed in the pockets of his hoodie. "I know. I've been on the clock."

"You're so full of it." She felt like telling him about the madam whose number she knew for a fact Grant had on speed dial. But she didn't. And she quickly dismissed from her mind the reason why: that Grant had many times discussed how critical it was that they never talk with anyone about what went on behind closed doors. How jobs could be lost or gained and money could be earned or taken away based upon whether that information was available for the public to consume. How in the end the most important acting job they could do had nothing to do with the screen. "Forget Grant. I want to hear about hummingbirds."

"What do you want to know?"

"I don't know. Why them, specifically?"

"You *are* into boredom." He paused and swirled the drink around in his hand. "Well, they're difficult to photograph. I can go a week without taking a decent picture." He sized up the photo she was looking at. Their shoulders touched. "A lot of other birds, you can see their personalities. Like with dogs, you can guess what they're thinking. But there's something strange about hummingbirds."

"They look like little aliens."

"Yeah. The way their plumage changes color depending on the time of day, the amount of light in the photograph, the angle. It's like trying to photograph a mirage. It's why I've kept this job for so long." He looked at her. "Ever seen the birds of paradise?"

"Maybe. Not sure."

"You need to." Ezra nodded toward his bedroom and they walked. He sat down at his desk and his back looked unusually straight and proper as he flipped open his laptop. The screensaver was gorgeous. It showed a bird capped with what resembled a bright turquoise hat, intersected by black curves, giving the appearance of stained glass. It also had a mustard sash protruding from its throat, bordered by a tomato-red felt. Then, below its feet, protruding out horizontally from its tail, were long black curlicues, shaped how an old silent film star might wax his long handlebar mustache.

"Crazy," she said.

He opened a folder on his computer and began flipping through more photos, each bird bizarre, brightly feathered, absurdly ornate. "Rainforest. South Pacific."

She imagined how they'd look on the big screen and wondered whether there was a way to get a movie set there, with the birds playing some sort of role that would feel organic. It would be tough, but some viewers loved these sorts of visuals almost as much they loved a good plot.

"I know," he said. "Why do they look like this? How does this happen?" He leaned in toward the screen. "The rainforest seems lush, but it's ruthless. Species have to grow weird adaptations to survive." The next one had a black oval mask with broad turquoise eyes and skinny little legs. The bird resembled a child's attempt at drawing a cartoon. Sybil glanced over at Ezra. He was so serious right now, like a little kid.

They scrolled through a few more pictures in silence. Maybe this was a way out: she could pitch a love story between a movie star and a groundskeeper-turned-nature-photographer. But to do it right, the travel budget alone would have to be massive. They'd have to find an angel investor who also happened to be a birder. And that would defeat the purpose, having a film. It wouldn't really be an escape.

"What's it like there?" she asked.

He exhaled and scooted back from the desk. "I wish I could tell you."

"These aren't yours?"

He shook his head.

"Why haven't you gone?"

"I don't know. I mean I could, right? Save up, buy a ticket. It just feels like there needs to be more to it than just *going*."

He shook his head and clicked to another picture. She couldn't read the look on his face.

For some reason she felt as though she'd played a part in his not going. She banished the feeling and squeezed his knee. "You need to go."

"I can't."

"Why?"

"The pool needs cleaning."

She laughed, and spotted a framed photograph on the desk of a young boy in a dark suit. The boy was clearly Ezra; even at that young age, he already had those deep eyes, the inklings of a sensitive jaw, and the posture of a surfer. Beside him stood a tall woman, dressed in a seafoam-green pantsuit with matching pumps and hat. Sybil could only assume this was his mother. She had Ezra's eyes, but the rest of her features weren't nearly so inviting—they were imposing, in fact, if not severe—but no, maybe it was just her expression, which—the longer Sybil looked at the photo—seemed to be one of weariness and fear. "Who's this?" she asked.

He clicked through another photograph on the computer screen and looked up. "Speak of the devil." He picked up the framed photograph and quickly set it back down. "If you really do want to understand why I haven't gone, well, she's the key."

Why was everyone's mom both crazy and the most important person in their life? "Let me guess: she was controlling."

"Yeah, but it was more than that."

"Manipulative?"

He chuckled and looked down, rubbing his temples. "What would you say if I told you people referred to my mother as the Prophetess?"

She glanced again at the picture again. "Bullshit."

"Doesn't look like a cult leader, does she?" He appraised her reaction then returned to the pictures. "But she was. One that deified birds, if you can believe it."

She didn't know what to say. Was this a joke? She looked at Ezra—who went back clicking through pictures on the screen—and felt a small twinge of fear. She realized that she didn't really know this man. Her reasons for trusting him were based on, what, how attractive he was? His skills at gardening? His willingness to cover her with towels when she'd blacked out after going on a bender?

But no, that was Grant talking—Grant who thought the worst of people, who assumed that everyone had ulterior motives. Ezra had never shown a single malicious sign in all the time she'd spent with him. "That might make bird photography complicated."

"They were everywhere growing up. Our house, the church, the school."

"Like as pets?"

"No, more like boarders. That part I loved. It made it less lonely. Building nests in light fixtures, stealing food, landing on your shoulder to lick the sweat from your hair."

"Wait. Birds actually lick?"

He laughed. "But you've got to understand that it didn't feel weird at the time, the church, the birds, my mom being a prophetess. Sometimes it still doesn't, because I was so close. It's not like I converted. I was born into it, so for a long time it was all I knew."

She wondered if she'd heard any stories about the cult and just didn't remember. She imagined news feeds from years back:

buildings on fire in Texas from a botched invasion, dark cabins in wooded mountains.

He pulled at his earlobe. His shoulders seemed to have slouched. "The people, her followers—those were the only people I knew. There was a school with the church. It was all we did." He took a deep breath. "I'm sorry, it's just been so long since I've talked about this. And I've never really talked about it."

"You don't have to," she said. His eyes had that glazed look. He wasn't listening. She wanted to hear more and she didn't. It was fascinating, and she was no longer scared. Ezra was a good person. Her intuition would have told her otherwise by this point. That said, learning all of this about him was beginning to make her feel diminished. She didn't know why. But it did.

"So it was completely insular," he said. "Suffocating. I was her little puppet. I don't believe she ever meant it to be that way, but it was. Front row left, every Sunday, there'd be a story about me, about how young and pure I was, how cute and earnest. Think of me as her walking, talking, sermon illustration. My life was her open book. She used to say I was living proof that the only father we needed was God in heaven. I don't know if I could even begin to explain to you what kind of pressure that puts on a kid.

"But the kicker is, when she wasn't at church, or at school, when we weren't expecting visitors at our house, she was a completely different person. Bottles of hard liquor. Pills. Strange men. Who knows what else." He clicked absently through some more pictures, fingers thudding into the keys. "And she'd cruise around naked, everywhere, all the time."

The silence was too uncomfortable. "Sounds like she knew how to party." It was out before she could stop.

He chuckled a bit. "Well . . ."

"I'm sorry, that just came out. I'm an asshole. This is real." She squeezed his knee.

He looked over and shrugged. "I know it's kind of crazy."

As he continued talking about his mother's church, she felt growing inside of her the same kind of discomfort as when Grant told her the scant bits and pieces of his own tragic childhood. Annoyed that her own childhood, filled with middle-class convention, was so easy to talk about, because it *was* relatively easy, and didn't stack up. She'd had so little to overcome—even if it often felt otherwise. She'd been raised well. Loved and cherished, challenged and taught. She should have been grateful. She *was* grateful, but here was the thing: her easy childhood made her feel shallow, because having an easy childhood made people think you were shallow. She'd never admit to believing this in public—she'd be crucified—but it was there, inside of her, a belief she couldn't shake: that the quickest path to success in the arts was claiming a childhood tougher than everyone else's.

Hadn't Grant flat out admitted that he'd once hired someone for a lead role over a far more talented actor because, as he put it, *these days the hurt puppy gets the most attention.*

And what was the worst that had happened to her? Sure, from the moment she transferred to that elite private arts school in Seattle to pursue drama, everyone seemed intent to put her in her place, and felt it their God-given responsibility to remind her that her physical appearance meant nothing in the grand scheme of things—nothing, except that she should be shunned from all social activity, made to feel like a pariah, and yes, she had no friends growing up, and yes, it all probably started because freshman year this asshole senior with a bias for edgy, Off-Broadway musicals had hung a Barbie doll from a noose outside of her locker when she hadn't wanted to go out with him, and yes, the administration didn't take the threat seriously, and yes, they placated her parents with the sideways compliment *everyone's just jealous of her looks*, and yes, all the rest of this upperclassman's disciples in the lower grades called her Barbie throughout the rest of her time in high school—and yes, it was even worse when she tried to go goth, and then granola, until she finally gave up and went back to shopping at J Crew—and yes, her parents and grandparents and everyone else asked her completely different questions about her future than they did her boy cousins because, well, she was beautiful and thus best fit as a trophy wife, and yes, she moved to LA in part because she wanted to finally live in a place where she wouldn't feel the need to apologize for that one fucking thing she couldn't control: her genetics.

But who on earth cared about all of that? In the end, there were two facts that excused her from receiving any and all empathy, even in LA: she was beautiful, and a movie star.

She had it *all*.

Sure.

But as Ezra continued talking about his difficulties, she checked herself for that flurry of thought. She and Ezra weren't in competition. This wasn't some contest. This is what she hated about Grant, his believing that all anyone did or said was a potential threat to his position. He would call this tryst a call for attention, or even self-sabotage, because—as he'd said before— *her place in society had been accepted by everyone except her.*

But no, this wasn't even on Grant. If only. Ezra's story wasn't about how she'd been wronged. She knew that. She needed to stop making every fucking thing about her. She just needed to fight it.

"No, I understand," she said. "This was your mother. Your mother! And she's getting hammered Saturday night and getting up Sunday preaching the opposite."

He took a deep breath and leaned back. "I remember once when I was asking her about who the hell my dad was, because she refused to tell me anything about how I was born. I think she liked to pretend I was the virgin birth or something. Anyways, she was sprawled out on the couch watching a sitcom, naked as usual. *Eden time* is what she called it. So I ask her for the thousandth time about my father and all of a sudden she gets angry and tells me to strip. I'm like, no. No way. But she's like, *strip now or you're never going to know a thing about him.*"

Sybil said nothing. She felt herself begin to move past that moment of inadequacy, and start to feel him. She slowly began to feel relieved of guilt. In one of her acting classes a teacher had described the process of becoming someone's story. You had to not just picture it, but hum it, like a song you were trying to learn by heart. If you learned the song well enough it would become your own.

"So I take off my clothes," he continued. "It's embarrassing, but that's how much I wanted to know about where the hell I came from. I'm ten and I strip down in front of her. Of course, the second I'm naked I have a boner. Worst thing you could possibly imagine. But she ignores it. She says to me, *Now grab ahold of some skin on your stomach.* So I do. *Feel that,* she says. *Now grab some of mine*, meaning her stomach fat, and I'm like, No. But she says *Don't be embarrassed. You came from inside there.*

"So I grab her skin with my fingers and she says, *Does it feel any different?* Like does her skin feel any different than mine. I shake my head and she says, *That's right. We're more alike than you'd like to think. You don't need a father. You don't need anyone. You've got your mother right here.*" Ezra adjusted his seat and dragged his fingers slowly through his scalp, and then scratched the back of his head.

The room felt still and abuzz at the same time. "I don't really know what to say."

He stood up and paced across the room toward the bed for a moment before turning. "At the same time, you know what's strange?" he said. "I think I liked her more as a mess than when she was busy being the Prophetess."

She nodded and, despite herself, for a moment considered the possibility of what it would be like to play Ezra's mother in a movie. It would be a dynamic role for an older woman. She wondered what Grant would think of it, whether he might get on board with something like that. Wondered who might play Ezra. Whether Ezra would be okay doing the story in the first place. She caught herself thinking this way and felt a brief flash of shame, dry in her stomach.

Ezra returned to his seat and sighed as he sat down.

"So, to your question," he said. "I went to my room after that and started doing push-ups and sit-ups to try to purge myself of what just happened. When I came back, she was passed out. Cigarette still smoking between her fingers, mouth open, snoring, teeth stained purple from wine. I felt I should stay there, just in case, you know. Anyway, the television still had one of her comedies on, so I sat down and changed the channel and stopped on this public television nature special. And there they were." He gestured to the screen. "Of all things, birds. But the most beautiful I'd ever seen. I sat there in the middle of our suffocating room, in the middle of our suffocating little world, and thought, *somehow, I've got to get there.*"

She thought of what a ticket would cost. It would be nothing for her to pay for it. She'd go with him, even. Finally a place, and a reason! She'd catch hell for it, but so what? He needed this and so did she.

"So, I moved halfway there. A quarter of the way. Across the country, East Coast to West. But to answer your original question, why haven't I been there yet. Well . . ."

"It's complicated," she said. It felt like to use any more words to try and encapsulate it for him would be cruel. There are places you can never leave. And then the question of what had kept her, and what was keeping her, with Grant. But forget all of that. They could go. They could be on a plane by maybe even tomorrow. "Then what happened?"

"What do you mean?"

"Did you up and leave right then?"

He chuckled and shook his head. "Not for years. The next morning, she didn't remember what happened. Or at least she didn't act like she could remember. But that's how we treated what happened when no one else was there."

Sounded familiar. She took both his hands and looked dead into his eyes. Would he go with her? She suspected yes. But could she actually go herself, or was this feeling inside of her just another act, when acting could feel so, so real. She dismissed the worry as fear. "You need to go. We need to go."

He opened his mouth as if he was trying to say something.

"I can buy the tickets. Cover expenses. It'll be easy to make up some sort of excuse." It felt so good to tell him this. She hoped it was true, that she could trust it.

"I couldn't—"

"I want this. I need some time away to figure stuff out, and this can be it." There she was, softening it. Making it easier for them both. It was the right thing to say, she told herself, to take the pressure off—he needed her to need it too.

He broke into a smile and his eyes clouded up. He laughed.

They embraced. She didn't want to let go. The wonder of the moment threatened to empty as they stood there. But it didn't. She almost couldn't believe it. This was real. Pure. They were going to seek out the truth because they wanted it for themselves, and for no other reason than that. God, she needed this.

She let go. Ezra was flushed, eyes wide. He looked to be taking short, shallow breaths. She thought for a moment he might cry, but then he brought his fingers to his neck and pressed into the skin.

"Are you okay?"

"Sometimes my body freaks out," he said. "It'll pass." He stood up and walked out.

She followed him through the front door.

"It can help just to walk around," he said.

A panic attack. She knew them well. Had had them on many a night, and on many a set, and had watched others go through the same. She wondered whether she'd done something to trigger it. But she took his hand and his grip was tight.

Outside, the morning sun was bright but not yet warm. The silence as they walked was peculiar. Maybe she'd never really heard it before; there was always a plane overhead, always the breeze, always an interruption every waking moment. Now it felt holy, if there was such a thing. People assumed intimacy was comfortable. Maybe it could be. But this wasn't like that, not quite. It was more that she felt alive in it. A live wire. Ezra's vulnerability . . . these weren't the things people shared with her. She met everyone at their most impressive, which was another way of saying most guarded. But this was that sharp edge of reality, where everything was buzzing, heightened. And Ezra, he was so broken, yet so full. Hands shaking. Body unable to hold what he had inside.

She saw a deep dignity in it. She wanted to see it through with him. They would buy plane tickets and fly away as soon as they could get a flight. She closed her eyes and they continued walking. Slowly, Ezra began to grow calm. A dry wind blew through the grounds and a plane overhead roared. They reached the north end of the property and now were circling back around through a row of lavender bushes that smelled like tea.

Then it was upon her. The scene became overwhelming. The drone of the hundreds of bees gathering pollen from the masses of lavender felt ominous. She felt the urge to check her phone but knew to do so would be terrible.

Ezra stopped. "You okay?"

"You're contagious," she said.

"I'm sorry—"

"No," she said. "I didn't mean that. I'm just going to head upstairs to take a bath. I think I need some time to just think."

It was the opposite though, wasn't it? She needed time not to think. Thinking never quieted her brain. It did the opposite—at times she even lost complete control of her thoughts, and she experienced what she could only describe as someone madly flipping channels in her brain from one image to the next, with no rhyme or reason to it, and all she could do was sit there helpless, waiting for it to stop. But this was only the damn withdrawal symptoms. That was all. In her pocket her phone buzzed.

"I'll see you in a bit," she said, and left him for the mansion. She peeked into her pocket; the text was from Grant. *Call me.* She ignored it. She would ride this out. She wanted a warm bath and some good music and a few magazines and a way to feel bright and good and that everything was under control, or at least would be soon. She walked toward the door and saw herself reflected in the glass. Her thoughts dug into her.

You're leading him on.

She opened the door and went inside.

Selfish. Narcissistic.

She started running up the stairs.

You're a fraud. Everyone knows it. Even your friends know it. They're just scared to say it because of Grant.

She got to the tub and turned on the water and sat down on the edge and began sobbing. Each and every terrible thought was voiced in a confident, chorus of godlike voices. Her anxiety and sorrow? Her plight? A farce in comparison to Ezra's and Grant's. She was a shallow pool compared to their oceans. A queen who everyone hated. She'd done next to nothing to deserve the crown, and she knew it, and everyone knew it, and nothing in the world could change it.

Goddamn these withdrawals. And Grant. She just needed to fight it. She wiped her nose and twisted the knob on the faucet back and forth, over and over, until she was making only the smallest changes. Minutes passed. She just couldn't find the right fucking temperature.

TEN

A few hours later they were back in the mansion, stretched out on couches, watching some trashy afternoon entertainment news program with the volume low. After the bath, she'd gone through her workout regimen and achieved a measure of balance she didn't want to give away. The bitter self-appraisal of earlier had quieted and she saw it for what it was: her old self, trying its best to gain back the ground it had lost over the last week.

Ezra had taken it all in stride. He was understanding. Incredible, even, especially in light of the trauma he'd obviously endured—but she absolutely *could not* allow herself to draw comparisons between her and him. To do so was stupid. Self-defeating. A habit contrary to how she wanted to live her life.

This was about being together and loving each other in the time they had together. Love didn't tally points. And Ezra was attractive—he understood intuitively what it meant to be an *other* in this particular way.

Which highlighted the problem with her and Grant. His otherness was won through grit, determination, and ruthlessness.

Everything was a competition. It had only worked for this long because he was always the winner, she the loser, and they were both comfortable with that.

Miserable, on her end, but comfortable.

Ezra hadn't mentioned the trip since he'd come inside, and she knew he wouldn't bring it up until she did. When it came to favors, he was clearly the sort of person that made you insist. That was what her parents would have called *polite*.

Her phone buzzed on the coffee table: Grant's number shadowed by a stock avatar. Her mind replaced it with an image of his cunning eyes and jaw.

Ezra glanced over and went back to the show.

She didn't reply to the text. Another quickly followed. *It's important*. She hated messages like that. So vague and manipulative. So anxiety producing. So typical.

Ezra's phone chimed. He took it out of his pocket and glanced at it for a few moments before putting it away. She wondered who might be calling. Was it Grant? Checking up on her? Maybe. But unlikely. And anyway, Ezra didn't respond. And she didn't feel comfortable asking, seeing as he didn't ask her, either.

The text could also have been from April, angling to get him back or still furious over what had happened. Beyond that, she didn't know. He hadn't really mentioned his friends. It occurred to her that this relationship was probably as much a break from his own life as hers was from her own. A reminder that under the current circumstances, they didn't exactly mesh. What, was he going to invite her out bowling with his buds? A double date with another of his groundskeeper friends?

She recognized that she felt threatened by whoever had texted him, and realized this was why the trip made so much sense.

Right now—so soon after connecting—it would be devastating for them to try to face the vast differences in their lives and respond to them with trust. To call class merely a social construct was like dismissing one of those marvels on Ezra's laptop as just another bird.

The television screen flickered to a line of makeup products she'd been passed over for as a possible spokesperson. The actor who'd gotten the role was fresh from starring in sitcoms for kids, and had the ability to pull in not only the younger crowd, but also the aging beauties. The latter all wanted what they once had. Sybil? She represented what they feared might happen to them.

She knew this wasn't quite true, but it'd felt that way when she'd received the news about the commercial, and here she was, sliding back into that mind-set again. Pretending she understood some casting director's decision when in reality she hadn't a clue; she'd just rather own the worst possible answer than hope for a better rejection, only to be disappointed.

If only knowing this meant more. If only when the epiphany struck she found herself changed. If only this realization wasn't one she had to come to over and over again.

She needed to stop thinking. When she started thinking she started feeling terrible. Was it Hamlet that said *There is nothing good or bad, but thinking makes it so*? This was one of those days that seemed bent on making her kneel. Or go fetal. She couldn't let it.

She sat up, crossed her legs beneath her, and turned off her phone. Then, as Ezra watched, she held it aloft between her finger and thumb and dropped it into the bright silver garbage basket next to the couch. The phone's impact was muffled by a firm bed of junk mail.

"Phone dead?" Ezra asked, peering over at her but still lying down on the couch as the television blinked through car commercials.

"I wish."

"Are you all right?"

This was why she liked him: he didn't ask *who was that?* even though she knew her gesture begged for that sort of attention. "I'm great."

He kept staring at her. "C'mon." He swung his feet off the couch so he was sitting. "What's up?"

She leaned back, feeling the warmth of emotion building in her neck, her ears. She was about to cry. But it wasn't a cry of panic. It was a good cry, the kind when someone actually wanted to understand you, even though you were a mess. Ezra wasn't going to treat her as some entitled prima donna for having the gall to say she was having a rough time. He'd at least proven that. He wasn't social media. He wasn't Grant. He wasn't, well, anyone. She choked out the words, "This is tough for me."

He came over and sat next to her and began rubbing her back as she cried. The celebrity news came back on. The thought occurred to her that this was how it could be. All of the shades open in every room. Vaulted skylights transparent, not tinted dark like Grant preferred them. Letting in sunlight. The peach paint on the far wall of the room, glowing. But forget this house; they could get one on the coast, right on the shore, like the one Grant had now but without the feel of a fortress.

A place in the South Pacific. An open-air bungalow, Ezra lying there, casual yet attentive. Engrossed in his photography and in their love life, which was free to blossom without harsh realities of the outside world. They'd stay for a few months. Who knew, maybe a few years. What difference was age thirty-eight compared to thirty-five? She'd probably return looking better than when she'd left, just from the lack of stress. Yes. They'd disappear. She'd lose her phone and her agent and the silence would no longer be oppressive, because it had been her choice.

She could be open. She could be free of all of this pent-up bullshit.

Then, finally, there would be a story. People would want to know why on earth someone so successful and so connected would leave the business, and she wouldn't tell them, she'd hold it over them like a secret only fit for ears who had been there, because hers was a reality that they never would nor could understand. And this? This would prove it. She would create a mystery and people would have to try and decipher it from her roles, which from then on would be more complex. A path towards reinvention: simply disappear. When she came back, she'd be changed, the world would be changed, and then she and Ezra could work out what to do next, on their terms.

"Okay," she said. "My birds of paradise . . ."

He was waiting there patiently, kindness in his eyes. What had she been doing with Grant all of these years?

". . . were all the important films I was going to make."

He scanned her face. "So you made it."

She searched his eyes to see if he was being sarcastic. He wasn't. He was trying to be polite. "*Important* films. But you're a gentleman."

He shrugged. "You've done well."

Was that what they were talking about? Doing well? She suddenly felt petty. "Listen to me," she said. "Complaining again."

"No. I didn't mean to. I mean, who am I to tell you how you should . . ."

"—No. It's fine. I know you weren't . . ."

"—I really hate it when people make assumptions, like I just did," he said.

They were staring at each other, both so serious, and then a smile broke across his face, and she felt one peel across hers, as well. They were laughing at themselves and each other at the same time. They were the same. Despite everything, the same. "I love you," she said.

He colored.

It had just come out, and though it had sounded impulsive, she realized she didn't feel nervous at all—she meant it. She remembered how nervous she was with Grant, wondering whether he loved her. When he'd finally said it, she'd felt as though she'd passed some sort of test. But this admission felt as natural as her lungs taking breath, and it was clear by Ezra's embarrassment that the notion had been pressing on his mind as well.

"I've never been in love before," he said.

She went to him and kissed him, hard, full. He tasted faintly of coffee.

His hands were around her and he pulled her close.

She pulled back from him and smiled.

He looked surprised.

"Don't worry. Just give me a sec." She slid her thin gray laptop over, flipped open the screen, and her plain blue desktop background lit up, document images scattered randomly across it. "I need to show you this."

"Cool."

She realized that he probably thought it was something fun. "This is serious, though."

"Serious."

"Very serious." She laughed. "No, I mean it. This is really important."

"This is your birds of paradise."

"Yes." She gave him a quick kiss, pulling his lip back with hers.

She took a deep breath and searched the web for the news site. For a moment, she felt a wisp of sentimentality from back a decade-plus, in her early days in Hollywood, before Grant, playing her favorite foreign film clips for some dull piece of pretty meat feigning interest in French cinema in hopes that he might get to fool around later. Even then she'd felt embarrassed, as though sharing her own desires was poor form, versus acquiescing to another's.

She found the clip and cued it up. "I'm not going to give you any context."

A female reporter, surrounded by storefronts resting beneath skyscrapers, talked into a foam-capped microphone.

Often assumed to be simply a third-world problem, acid attacks over the last few years have been on the rise in some major cities . . .

The camera swept over a huge, modern city, then streets teeming with people and cars and storefronts.

. . . women have been especially targeted, some on charges of immodesty, others out of jealousy. For instance, this woman, who requested that we withhold her name . . .

And there she was. Helen. Sybil had seen the face on this video countless times, but it never ceased to affect her. A sad warmth grew in her stomach. The newscast showed a picture of Helen before it happened: mouth wide, perhaps afraid to smile, lips thin and serious but beautiful in their soft lines. Her nose was long and slender, like her chin, and her thick black locks draped all the way down past where the picture cut off at her shoulder. Sybil had yet to find an actor who might be able to capture her features, though every time she saw someone similar on the street, she would stop and stare. There had been a singularity to Helen's proportions, the way they seemed to lean this way and that, the way they appeared to stretch just a bit farther than was common.

. . . *she allowed her roommate to photograph her in suggestive poses while studying for a semester overseas in the States . . .*

Sybil glanced at Ezra, who was intent on the screen. For some reason, she felt like stopping the video before it could get to the next part, and just explaining it away.

. . . *she returned home from overseas changed. She no longer wanted to marry and pursue domestic life; she wanted to return to the States to get an advanced degree in economics. The son of a well-known family in her community proposed, and she declined. Then, for reasons unknown, the picture surfaced, and the family of her suitor retaliated . . .*

Helen, now deformed, appeared. She had a cream white mask, not unlike those one might wear for a Greek tragedy, completely covering her face. But then she took it off and showed what was left below. Her face had melted from the acid. It shined in places where it shouldn't, a plastic glare in the light. Sybil shivered and wrapped her arms around her stomach. There were a few places where she could go in her mind and immediately conjure tears, should she need them for a part. This was one.

"My God," said Ezra.

Helen spoke. Her voice sounded painful to produce, grating, like a broken wind instrument.

There is an understanding you get about people, that maybe many people know, but that I didn't. The love of some people is immense, as is the hatred. I feel that for many years I was swimming along the top of such things, that I didn't understand them, because I had no cause to understand them. There is a current beneath, and it is strong in both directions.

Helen stopped for a moment. The camera panned out to show her full body. A hand from off screen reached over and held hers.

There is no room for modesty now. I would never have said this before: I was beautiful. It would have been better had I not been beautiful. Or at least it would have been much simpler.

Helen paused for a moment and took her hand back from whoever was offscreen.

This? she said, meaning her face. *This threatens people, as did how I looked before. There are many different kinds of power.*

Sybil paused the clip. They were silent. "What do you feel?"

She watched as Ezra took a deep breath from the couch. He leaned over his crossed legs and rested his cheeks in his hands. He was still staring at the screen. "I don't even know."

When Grant had seen it, he was affected, but with disgust. There are some reactions you can't hide. And when she'd pushed him on what else he felt, he became angry and made her feel as if she was accusing him of something. *You can't spring this sort of thing on me and expect me to be a certain way,* he'd said. And she'd replied, *I forgot. Only you're allowed to do that.*

Sybil clicked shut the browser and shut the laptop. "There are three story lines. The first, of course, is the woman, Helen. Her thread will focus on the power her beauty gave her, and what she was able to experience because of it, and what she could not. How the fact that she was beautiful kept her relationships at a particular tenor. She said that she floated on top. If she'd just stayed home and accepted her life, would she have been happy? Perhaps ignorant, but genuinely happy?"

Ezra leaned back.

"The second story line is the guy who proposed to her. His power is inherited, but because his family is dependent on his future success and standing for their current and future well-being, he also has a firm destiny to follow. So, we'll outline the slow degradation of his independence as an individual, and the formation of his identity as a person groomed to act not in his own interest, but his family's. He didn't want to do it, the acid. And in fact, if there was any envy in him, it wasn't over some other man that might one day have her. He was envious of the fact that Helen could act so freely. He didn't want to have her as much as he wanted to *be* her.

"The final thread is the American doctor. She's beautiful, white, well-educated, and from an affluent background. But she's miserable. She could have made millions doing plastic surgery but she's always had this nagging sense that she didn't deserve what she had. So now she lives in a foreign country making next to nothing at a nonprofit. But years have gone by, and the tragedy of the women she helps doesn't mean to her what it used to. She's grown numb; plus, she's terribly lonely. Men aren't comfortable with her and women are threatened by her. What makes her such a powerful woman, what allows her to rise, are also the things that keep her from any real intimacy. And now she's grown envious of the women she treats, of their tragedies. She pities them but she's also jealous. And she hates that as well. But most of all, she's haunted by the fact that her own story isn't a story anyone would ever want to hear. The story of power, privilege, and the loneliness it has caused."

Ezra tapped his finger on his lips.

"Here's how it ends. After the tragedy, many of these women give up. They can't come to terms with all that they've lost, all they'll never have again. Helen—the woman you saw—ended up being one of those women.

"But there are others. Some of the women, once they've been stripped of their external beauty, develop these intimate, affectionate relationships, the depth of which they'd never come close to experiencing before. Some of them even confide that it might have been a deliverance, what happened. They feel free."

"But is that freedom?" asked Ezra.

"Exactly," she said.

Ezra sat there in silence. He closed his eyes and nodded, then gave her a small smile that told her he understood.

She felt warm, and shrugged. Embarrassed, but in a good way.

"And you're doing this movie?"

She took a deep breath. "No. It's locked up with Grant. Has been now for years. I wrote the screenplay and I'm supposed to have the part of the doctor, as well as direct. I never had the chance to meet Helen before she passed. But I've met multiple times with her family, and they've read it. They're waiting too."

Ezra paused. "So—"

"I don't know what to do." She looked down at her hands and began spinning the ring around on her finger. "There's really not much I can." She'd given Grant the rights in good faith. Back then they were a team, so she'd thought nothing of it. But in the time since, he'd done nothing. With this movie, she figured she'd finally be able to segue from starlet back to serious actor, as well as a director of serious films. All the interviews, the red carpet galas, the parties . . . she would no longer have to fake it and pretend that her roles were interesting, meaningful, anything other than shallow moneymakers for her and the studios and the investors.

But it was more than just her career. It was the opportunity to do right by Helen's family, by Helen. To feel as though what she was doing meant something other than just the usual hope for profits and acclaim. To feel good about herself. It was everything, dovetailed together.

"What's Grant waiting for?" Ezra asked.

She shrugged. In her mouth were the excuses she could make for him. Ones he'd made. Ones she'd repeated to herself like mantras. How the timetable for the movie wasn't perfect. Or that the script needed revising. Or that this actor's schedule or the situation at whatever studio wasn't right. And so on. She'd gone along with the delays, at first because she wanted to. Back then her star had been so bright that she didn't need him—or this movie—like she did now.

"He *could* make it happen," she said. "But he won't."

"And he knows what it means to you?"

She said nothing.

"That's bullshit."

"Yes. But I'm trapped."

"Couldn't you just—"

"—You don't know how it works." She felt like kicking Ezra. She'd been obsessing over possible answers for years and what, he was going to snap his fingers and conjure some solution out of nowhere? "I'm tied to him. No worthwhile producer's going to touch a project of mine without his nod, and I'm not going to let it die on the festival circuit."

They sat there for a moment. She felt his arms around her. At first she stiffened at them. She felt angry. But she slowly relaxed. Ezra cared. That's why he'd tried to offer help. He just didn't understand. And it felt so good to be held. She felt free to cry, and began to do so in earnest. The more you wanted something, the more that yearning hurt, and the more difficult it was to trust people with the knowledge of that burning desire in your being. People praised desire and ambition, but sometimes it felt like an affliction, or even a disease.

She remembered the moment she'd caught it. She was driving home from her opening night performance at the community theater, away from that caustic drama department at her high school, where at eighteen she'd just finished playing Masha in *Three Sisters*. And she'd killed it. Killed it!

On the way home, all of the streetlights seemed to turn green upon her approach, the neon signs in the shop windows seemed to shine just for her, and even the jerk who cut her off at the intersection must have been, in her mind, on his way to something important. She kept the stereo off and drove in silence because her insides still hummed with a pleasure she didn't wish to dampen. It wasn't just the sound of the applause, but also the look of people applauding once the house lights went up. Even now, years later, she could remember hoping the warm feeling would never wear off.

The words they'd used about her performance: impressive, amazing, stunning. The words they'd used about her: beautiful,

gorgeous, magnetic. These were the women, of course—the men
blushed, maybe nodded in agreement, their manner expressing
what words couldn't.

She felt it would sound trite to admit how much the recep-
tion meant. She'd downplayed it then, as if the performance
itself was everything and it didn't matter if people were even
there. The truth? She was won over at that theater, both by the
rush of performing and the praise she received afterward. And
the email she received from an agent a few days later, asking her
to fly to Los Angeles to meet, made every last taunt by the idiots
at her high school feel silly and desperate.

But it was strange, and perhaps this was the real cost that
Grant could never understand: she could never remember anything of her performances themselves. It was as if they were
erased from her memory. She came to the conclusion that the
act itself must be some sort of sacred space. When entering into
someone else's skin, even someone imaginary, you were only
allowed that present feeling of the moment. You could get lost
in it, but you couldn't return to it afterward and experience it
again. It stood alone, the time.

"What are you going to do?" Ezra asked.

Could she really leave it behind? The shitty roles, yes. But
that wasn't what he was asking. Could she really leave behind
the possibility of doing Helen's movie? Could she leave behind
the possibility of losing herself in a part that meant something to
her? That would provide for her the admiration of an audience
she'd been yearning to receive for so long? The gratefulness of
a family who'd lost their daughter, and yearned to see the tragedy of her life teach others? A possibility to begin directing and
acting in meaningful films on a regular basis?

She looked at her phone in the trash. Silent, except for the occasional annoying prod by a cold husband who'd long ago ceased finding value in his wife. She exhaled. "We need to pack."

He shook his head. "This is so unbelievably strange."

"I know."

He blinked. "Yes, all of this, of course, but there's more."

"What do you mean?"

He rubbed his forehead. "I have one more story about my mother. I hate to put it on you, but it's . . . I don't know."

"It's okay. Just tell me." She rubbed his shoulders.

"When I was fourteen, my mother burned herself alive."

ELEVEN

By morning the bliss of the night before had faded into a surreal anxiety. The further into the city Sybil drove, the more the sun seemed to glare. She palmed the wheel and guided her convertible into the parking lot of the offices of her agent.

She didn't know what to make of what little Ezra had managed to tell about his mother's self-immolation, and she hadn't the heart to push him for details of the event itself. But she did ask how it had affected him all of these years. Instead of answering, he began speculating about why his mother had done it. *She felt trapped. Ashamed. Cursed. She was tired of hiding—so many years of being the Prophetess had worn on her. She wanted the world to know her pain. She wanted the world to know her. So she tried to tell them, the only way she felt she could.*

In short, he'd divulged what little he could bear to—and it was far more than she had a right to expect. For that, she was grateful. More and more, this insane trip seemed to make sense for them both—they could get away and talk through all of this shit, carry each other's burdens, and maybe come out from it less fearful and inhibited.

She'd bought the plane tickets. One way. The feel of clicking the purchase tab was both thrilling and heavy. The earliest reasonably direct flight would leave in three days, which felt like an eternity to wait, though she realized it was still nowhere near enough time to tie up loose ends and pack. But when you made a decision like this, the last thing you wanted was more time to stew, because there was always something pulling you back to where you were before. People who ask why nothing ever changes, she thought, don't recognize the power of the familiar. So quiet, so subtle, yet always coercing you back to where it started.

She'd had a stress dream the previous night, a variation of one she'd had many times, before big auditions, meetings, premieres. In the dream, she soared high above the coastline, arms like wings, wind stiff and hot and dusty against her belly and face, making her eyes and mouth parched. She was up north in wine country, following the coastal highway south along the water. Acres of parched canyons flanked her left side, their folds peppered with vineyards and the occasional pathetic tree, slouching up from the ground like a knobby finger. The whole of it threatening to burn.

But to her right swirled the ocean, an impossible richness of water for thousands of miles, getting deeper every day with each melting glacier. Every shade of blue and green, waves curling around points, lines of swell appearing out of the deep, kelp out past the breakers, seals bobbling, humpbacks slapping their tails.

That the desert and the ocean could be so near each other, so close, touching even, yet never really mix—it made almost no sense.

She soared over Grant's property on the coastline, and soon the city began to appear, first as a denser scattering of houses, then more, until finally it was a thick, relentless storm of commerce. The scene reminded her of the time as a kid when she'd gone to a museum to see a steam engine—the pipes, the tubing, the gears, all of it so thick and precise and beautiful that she caught herself holding her breath while watching it work.

She flew over a golf course, over an interchange, over palm-lined streets. She neared her neighborhood and could see the streets branching off from the main causeways, each diminishing until they were only small tributaries, climbing up hills into larger estates with pools. Then there was the rental home, that sixteenth-century manor house on the hillside, and she was flying down, descending. Suddenly she spotted a body on the patio, laid out like a chalk drawing, and before she could identify it, she woke.

It was Ezra. She could feel it in her heart. And not only that, she'd done it.

But it had only been a dream. It occurred to her that the body made perfect sense, in light of her stress. She had reason to be worried about him. For one, worry was one of the many prices you paid for love. Second, Grant at some point would find out, if he hadn't already.

Not that she had any reason to believe that Grant would do anything violent. But there was always a threat about him. You couldn't be or stay in his position without it. That sense of being above the political skirmishes—that when it came down to it he would do what he had to do, no matter what stood in the way.

Regardless, would Grant really care, as in care about *her*, as in be angry at the affection she and Ezra had shared? Would he be protective of their marriage because, say, he valued it outside of how it served his personal ambitions? She felt silly that even just yesterday, after Ezra revealed Grant's proposal to spy on her, she'd let herself believe it. Even felt flattered by the prospect.

She'd seen Grant furious with envy, but only toward people who were in some regard more powerful than him. This affair? There was a category for this, an obvious one, and Grant loved categories, because they allowed him to dismiss the urges behind people's motives as common and therefore of little interest. He'd call Ezra the cabana boy and her the tragic starlet and have a good laugh at how predictable they both were, and feel more powerful because of it. He would wrap the affair in old newspaper, place it inside a packing box, and store it away, perhaps only occasionally bringing it out as an anecdote to share at luncheons to prove how little even the most personal of relationships meant to such a big man like him.

Then again, he might hide it even tighter than she had! Making it into a big deal could make him appear weak, and Grant would rather die than have that happen. To preserve his ego and machismo in business dealings, he might even out one of his mistresses, inform the press that he and Sybil had been seeing other people for quite some time, that they'd been in a de facto open relationship for years, that they'd always admired the French for their lack of puritanical hang-ups.

But no, he wouldn't even do that, because philandering could stand in the way of a future election. If he couldn't bury it, he'd talk about it in passive, political terms. Irreconcilable differences. Opinions were made clear. Goals were diverging, so decisions were made. Paths were taken.

Whatever it took to stay above the fray.

Likely, it would be anticlimactic, Sybil told herself. She and Ezra would be fine. Still, she was having trouble catching her breath and her hands were shaking as she sat in the car outside her agent's office, and the AC just couldn't break through the heat because the top was down and the smoked glass of the office doors reflected the sun onto her face.

It would be fine. This wasn't about what Grant thought, what the press thought, social media, her parents, her fans, her critics. It was about what she *knew*, which was that she needed something different.

She stepped out of the car into the dry, hazy sun.

A few paparazzi rushed through the hedges from the sidewalk. They began snapping pictures. "Sybil, we hear your marriage is on the rocks. Care to comment?"

She hurried past them and up the steps in silence. She briefly wondered if they knew something, imagining that perhaps someone had snuck onto the property and photographed her and Ezra together. But she dismissed it as just a stupid paparazzi tactic to get her to engage. Either way, who cared? It was over now, wasn't it? She didn't owe anyone anything.

She pulled on the handle; the hushed opening of the brass-lined doors always made her feel sentimental, though she quickly stifled the feeling, fearing it might hinder her resolve. The office hadn't changed since the seventies. The walls were still dressed in fake wood paneling and the ceilings were fitted with Tiffany glass fixtures. The air smelled of potpourri. This was no accident. Other agencies strove to look cutting-edge, but not Pam's. Grant had once said after a few highballs of gin that the reason Pam was so successful was that she recognized the moment she changed from being an up-and-comer to being part of the establishment. There came a point you needed to own your status and relax into your privilege, or else people wouldn't ever stop thinking of you as up-and-coming—and you can only be an up-and-comer for so long.

There was a point where hustling began to work against you. A point where you had to sit and wait and let it come. If you're always out knocking on clients' doors you'll never be there to open your own.

Sybil walked in and saw that the administrative assistant was new, but like the upholstery, dressed for a different time. She was wearing a sixties bellhop vest and bouffant of professionally done fake red hair, striking Sybil as the type who might judge an apartment's feng shui while mispronouncing the term.

The admin smiled. Sybil hit her with a glare and perched on the arm of a brown sofa. She thumbed through the first few pages of an industry mag and closed it. Why had she glared? The woman was no threat. This was only more proof that she needed to leave. No wonder nobody would give her a part, if even the fucking secretary made her caustic.

The woman at the desk glanced up and said, "Pam is ready to see you now."

Sybil walked to the entryway and felt a tinge of bright, tinny desperation: she'd been so sheltered over the past week, and the rest of the world had kept moving on without her. But no. That didn't matter anymore.

Pam's office was nearly the size of a squash court, but felt much smaller because of the stacks of scripts, manila folders, and scribbled scraps of paper crowding every tabletop, chair, and bookshelf.

"Hey," Pam said, a tiny microphone wrapped around her tight, shiny, recently lifted chin. Her hair was silver when it had been brown a month ago. She nodded to take a seat.

Sybil relaxed into one of those modern chairs whose pad seemed nothing more than hard wax. "Give me some good news."

"Do you need it?" Pam asked, feigning concern for her well-being, or perhaps it was real concern, and the recent face-lift had kept it from appearing.

"Don't we all?"

The phone on her desk rang and she put up a finger for Sybil to wait as she answered it on her headset.

While Pam talked on the phone, Sybil pulled out her own and pretended to be engrossed in some deep conversation with a lover. She wet her lips with her tongue and made herself blush then wiped a stray bang from her brow like a schoolgirl who, after years of being ignored, was finally worth the effort of her older brother's friends.

She glanced up and saw that Pam was eyeing her. She thought the manipulation was working, but then Pam got up from her desk and stood and faced the window.

Why, Sybil thought, *am I doing this*? She slipped her phone into her purse. Hadn't her plan been to just tell Pam the truth? To be honest and forthright and leave on good terms? This wasn't who she wanted to be. Pam wasn't the problem. She was her ally, the one who'd always tried to have her interests in mind.

Pam turned back around and leaned against the window.

Sybil smiled at her and tried her best to mean it.

Pam told whoever was on the phone that she needed to call them back. Then she reached below her desk and handed over a slim stack of papers. "I have some new scripts for you to read."

Sybil crossed her legs and thumbed through them. Just the titles themselves screamed leftovers. Half of them were sequels of sequels. "Anything good?"

"There's decent money to be made in that stack."

Sybil took a deep breath. "Pam, I'm leaving."

Pam blinked. "I'm really surprised to hear you say that. You get the best parts that cross my desk. I promise you that."

It occurred to Sybil that Pam thought she meant that she was seeking other representation. "No," she said. "Let me clarify. I'm not leaving you. I'm leaving the business."

Pam stared at her for a moment. "You're not serious."

Sybil shrugged. "I've had enough."

"I know that it has been a little lean."

"More than a little."

"The parts will come."

"Will they?" Sybil stared her down.

Pam sighed and looked down, rubbing the bridge of her nose. "Fine. I don't know if the kind you're hoping for will. And if they do, I don't know when."

It felt as though she had been released. Her shoulders relaxed. "Thank you for being honest with me."

Pam shook her head and smiled, as if surprised, yet at the same time, not. "So where are you going?"

"Does it matter?"

Pam stood up and held out her hand. "Most likely not."

Sybil shook it. "Just deposit my checks as they come. I'll be in touch." She felt a lightness. One step closer to freedom.

The phone rang on the desk. Pam glanced down. "Hold on a second," she said to Sybil, and adjusted the headset mic back to her lips. "You'll never guess who's in my office."

Grant. "I really should go," Sybil said.

Pam picked up the phone and held it out. "He says it's an emergency."

Sybil searched her face. She didn't appear to know anything about anything. Fuck. This was the last thing she wanted to do now, in one of the last places. But she was stuck. She held out her hand and pressed the phone to her ear.

"Yes?"

"Hello, my darling."

That voice, the sound of a scythe through sand. There was rustling in the background and she could hear his breath. He was walking in a crowd. "Where are you?" she asked.

"I just got off a plane in JFK. The flight was miserable. I sat next to an investment banker from Dallas who was under the impression that derivatives were interesting."

"What are you doing in New York?" She glanced up. Pam mouthed her a question, pointing to the door, *would you like me to step out for a moment?* Sybil nodded, grateful. She heard the door close behind her.

"I think the more pressing question," Grant asked, "is why you haven't been answering the phone."

She didn't know what to say. Did he know about Ezra? She had no reason to think that he would. Though now that Grant was right there on the phone, she realized how thin that assumption was. She cleared her throat. "I haven't wanted to talk to you."

"You're talking to me now."

"Pam told me it was an emergency. That's beginning to seem like a stretch."

He took a deep breath. "Listen. I know how I've been lately. Or perhaps how I've been for a long time. And I understand why you would step out."

There was a pause. He still might not know. This could be bait. "I don't know what you're talking about."

"The gardener?"

"What about him?" She looked at the door to make sure it was closed. "He's got a girlfriend. April or something."

"April or something. I didn't know you guys were pals."

She felt the urge to tell him all she knew about *his* women.

"Look, I know," he said. "And it's fine. I'd already guessed it was happening."

"You're paranoid."

"Sybil, let's stop pretending. I have the security cameras connected to my phone. You had to have at the very least guessed that."

It occurred to her what this told Grant. Hell, what it told her. Such a massive oversight, to engage in an affair in one's own rental mansion while her controlling husband was away. She'd reasoned herself into being less careful after Ezra had told her that Grant had asked him to spy. Looking back, it made no sense. It was as if she wanted it to happen.

"Hello?" Grant said.

She looked around the office at all the scripts, the photos on the wall—some of which she was in—the movie posters, playbills. The apple cinnamon scent of this office, which she'd first stepped into as an insecure eighteen-year-old afraid to believe that she actually deserved to be here. Or forget the office—this neighborhood, this town, this zip code, this state. The sun, the palm trees, the fashion, the stupidity, the mindless, soul-sucking beauty of the place. Truth was, she loved it. It would be hard to leave, even knowing that after a few years, she'd come back. Hell, even the fucking paparazzi outside, as annoying as they were, wasn't their attention also proof that this was where she belonged?

"Sybil?"

And suddenly she knew. This affair wasn't just love. Neither was her being found out simply an oversight. It couldn't be. She was too smart to be this dumb. Somewhere, deep down, a part of her had been working this entire time to sabotage things with Grant. To sabotage her career. To sabotage her current life. And if that meant falling in love with the gardener, and blinding her to the obvious, so be it.

"Are you there? Hello?"

What else was that subterranean part of her up to? What other plans was it hatching? The mind was a fucking congress, using every backchannel to serve its agendas.

"I'm sorry," she replied, and cleared her throat. "I was simply going over my notes on all of your other women."

He laughed. "Thank you. Now we are talking like a real married couple."

"Go fuck yourself." She picked up a pen from Pam's desk and began clicking the point in and out.

"Listen. Let me speak plainly. I could say a lot of things. Lay out for you how I've been ignoring you and apologize.

Maybe we can talk about those things in depth at some point if it would help. But you know me, Sybil, better than anyone. I'm a bull. A first-rate asshole. I don't let anyone stop me. It's how I've always been. And it's served me well. Us well. But that's not okay when you're getting neglected, when my wife is the one that's having to always make do."

"Oh please." Did he actually think she'd buy that? He was such a manipulative fucking child. She walked over to Pam's window and scanned the busy street.

"I'm not lying. I've been trying to think about this from your perspective, put myself in your shoes, etcetera etcetera. Of course you stepped out. In fact, I'm surprised it took you this long."

"Even when you're trying to be nice, you manage to be condescending."

He laughed. "So true. But it's what you used to love about me. Maybe still do, if you'd give me another chance. But I have a gift for you. Something to prove it. Do you have your phone on you?"

"Why?"

"Check your inbox."

She wedged the landline between her shoulder and neck and dug into her purse. She cued up her messages and there was one from him with an attachment: a spreadsheet for some project called *Face*. She scrolled through the pages. "What is this?"

"Your film."

"Bullshit." She scrolled back to the beginning. He wasn't lying. She felt dizzy and leaned against Pam's desk.

"I'm in Manhattan meeting with a group of investors. I know how much you've wanted it. All these years. And I've neglected doing it. I've thought about it. Believe me, I have. But I've been selfish."

She could feel herself getting choked up. "Fuck you." But she was already imagining the opening scene of the film, with Helen in her dormitory room, taking those innocent photographs with her friends. She was already imagining the sounds of Helen's mother when she heard the news. She was already walking up the red carpet to the podium, acceptance speech shaking in her hands. "I'm so fucking pissed at you."

He laughed. "I'll take that as a yes. My flight arrives tomorrow at six p.m."

TWELVE

Late that afternoon, Sybil tried to forget about what she was doing and what she was going to do, and for a while succeeded. She locked the doors and set the alarms and pulled the shades tight. She shared a bottle of decade-old 98 point Chardonnay with Ezra and they made love slowly, methodically, as if savoring a beautiful passage in a novel. Then, spent, they propped their heads up on pillows and watched through the oriel window airplanes flying across the sun-scorched evening horizon.

Sybil unwrapped her legs from Ezra and sat up, back facing him. Her stomach churned a bit. She'd gorged herself on the wine, cheese, and olives. Her high was fading and she was beginning to feel guilty about both the food and Ezra, but then she remembered what was going to happen, and who she was, and what she and Grant had in store for the future, and how little bearing Ezra had in all of this. How lovely, but how short and insignificant their time together had been. After a few years, he would see this, and when he looked back, he would be grateful, and he would have a fun story to tell at parties, with a sly look of pride on his face.

It would never have worked. She'd been a fool, of course, as was her fault, as an artist: to believe the impossible. Their paths had wonderfully converged, but they were traveling in opposite directions—always had and always would. She'd always taken issue with that famous quote from Gatsby or whatever about the rich being different from everyone else, but maybe it was right, and it had only taken her until now to realize it. She stood and walked to the bathroom.

"What's wrong?"

She stuck her head around the corner. "Nothing."

"This feels different."

"What's different?"

"All of this."

His earnest look unnerved her. "I'm just tired." She ducked back into the bathroom and grabbed a towel. What was it Grant always said, that the most important acting job they could perform had nothing to do with the screen?

Ezra walked in after her. "Are you okay?"

She propped herself up on the counter and quietly sighed. It was, in the end, unfortunate, that when you closed a door, it wasn't just eliminating what you'd planned, but everything else that might have happened afterward. In another life, it could've been good with Ezra. "I'm not going with you."

He blinked.

"The ticket is yours. You should go. In fact, you need to go. And next week you'll find a substantial deposit to your bank account."

"I don't understand."

"Ezra, you are brave. So much more so than I am."

He took a step back and leaned against the doorframe. "What happened?"

"I don't know," she said. "It wasn't any one thing. And it definitely wasn't anything that you did. I just realized—"

"—he's coming back, isn't he."

She could explain herself, say that it wasn't about him, it was about this film. She could soften it: tell him that she was tied to Grant for as long as the film was in production, but once it came out, *maybe* they could take it up again, because at that point, *maybe* she wouldn't need Grant anymore, and she'd finally be free to do what she pleased. But no: to even leave open the door of possibility would be cruel. It would only lead him on, and she'd done that enough already. "He's back tomorrow."

Ezra said nothing. Just stood there and looked at her, eyes impossibly direct. It was terrible to see. She wanted him to say *fuck you*, break a lamp, the mirror. Even a slap would be better than the look on his face.

"You'll have to get your things," she said.

"You don't mean it." He walked over and took her wrists. "What's he making you do?"

She tried to pull free. "What are you talking about?"

He pushed her away. "All this bullshit about him being an asshole. Treating you like a piece of property."

"You need to go."

"Sybil, we can leave now. We can just go. I can protect you."

She started laughing, couldn't help herself. "Protect me? You think this is about protection?"

"He has to know." He looked young again, surprised. Like the first time she'd met him.

"Of course he knows," she said.

His face blanched. "I don't understand—"

"Ezra, leave," she said. "Now."

He gathered his clothes. "Keep the money. Keep the tickets, too. I don't want them."

She didn't argue. His footsteps echoed as he descended the spiral staircase. A host of emotions overwhelmed her. Relief that it was over. Guilt for how she had ended it. Even a bit of fear over what Ezra would do now that she'd set him free.

Most of all, she was ashamed. She couldn't unsee that look on his face. But maybe that was simply the cost of life for someone like her. Maybe, she thought, seeing those sorts of looks were what would make her artistry more complex. Ezra, and her parents, and most everyone else in their simple lives could avoid it, but people like her and Grant weren't afforded that luxury.

And there were worse feelings than shame. She could be ashamed and still wake up and greet the day. She could be ashamed and still smile and move and feel. She could be ashamed and make movies, garner awards—still act as though she weren't, and no one would know the difference, and even some of the time, she might believe it, too. It was, after all, just a feeling.

And speaking of feelings: love? Who was she kidding? Love had never been a real possibility for her. From the time she was a little girl, that—if nothing else—had been clear.

Other girls—the less pretty, the less talented, the less intelligent, the less at ease—they were to be loved. Her destiny was to be admired. It was time she accepted it.

She wiped her face, blew her nose, and returned to the bedroom. She slid open the drawer to her nightstand and removed Grant's green-and-white contact lens holder. She screwed off the top of both sides and poured the white powder onto a round, gold-rimmed vanity mirror, like she'd watched him do so many times before. To a new era. Two islands in a glassy lake.

THIRTEEN

Ezra checked his phone and only ten minutes had passed since she'd left the house to who knew where. It was probably foolish to stay, but he couldn't help but hope that Sybil had changed her mind, and there was the chance that something was wrong that he didn't know about. He continued pacing the lawn, already nostalgic about the groves of flowers—cool cream, bright buttercup, and hot vermillion—and standing guard, as always, the soft phallic bends of the palm trees, capped with their brittle flags—all here to witness to what would happen next. Their rustling and chattering unnerved him. He'd have to leave them behind, too.

But he still had this feeling. Maybe he was a fool. Maybe he was in denial. But it didn't make sense that what he and Sybil shared could change this quickly. And if, in the end, it *could* change this quickly, it might just as quickly change again.

He went inside the pool house and paced the kitchen, alternating sips between a beer and a glass of tap water. He used the restroom. Returned and watched. Used the restroom again. Returned. Checked his phone. He'd texted Bryce, with no response. Maybe payback for the way he'd ghosted over the last week—Bryce had messaged him a few times and he hadn't responded. He hadn't known what to say about April, nor had he wanted to try and bridge the gap between his old world and this new one. Especially considering he hadn't known what this was, yet. And to put words to it felt disloyal to the private existence he and Sybil were enjoying.

On the couch sat his packed bags. Even they seemed restless, on the verge of sliding off the cushions of their own volition. Had this past week not been the most miraculous of his life? Was that not worth the price of being played for a fool? No, it only made it worse. And funny how the sex, after all these years of waiting, ended up feeling almost crass compared to the companionship, the honesty, the openness.

There'd been a peace. Hadn't there? But now, as he thought about it, he wondered how on earth his mind could have come to such a conclusion. Peace? His emotions had been racing all week, between exaltation and anxiety. She'd seen only one of his panic attacks. He'd had several each day, mostly as he was landscaping, brought on by the feeling that all of this was sinful on a level he'd never before experienced. He'd slept with his neighbor's wife. In early biblical times his life would be at risk. Sybil's more than his.

His mother had slept with lots of men. He couldn't ignore that. But did that justify what he'd done with Sybil? Unlike his mother, he couldn't claim to have prophesied events and healed dozens of people. All he'd done was lie and hide.

But now he wasn't even sure about that. Over the last week, he'd gone over his history and motives countless times. Was he courageous for finally stepping out of his self-imposed seclusion of shame, or was his courage that of Adam biting the apple?

Did it make a difference?

He paced. Outside the kitchen window, the twilight wrapped everything in a sleepy haze. Glow from the bottom of the pool slithered up through the water. The beauty distracted him. But his brain soon returned to the mess: if only his mother had simply woken that one morning, called her dream with the doves peculiar, and gone on with her day, then most likely none of this would have happened. She would never have become the Prophetess. He would never have become the pathological mess that he was now.

She might still be alive, had she dismissed that dream. God, one small decision, based on the tiniest of thoughts, could project so far into the future. It could drive you crazy. Make you want to cling to a higher power.

But that was the thing. So long as you kept on living, you were choosing from the moment you rose each day. To act or not to act—both were choices, both were actions, both had consequences. He could see it now. All of the times he'd said no had really been their own kind of yes.

All of this was too much to think about. He wanted to be back in Sybil's bed, underneath her, feeling her warmth, listening to her breath, feeling the pulse of her heart. But the mansion was still empty. No light shone in any of those grandiose checkered windowpanes of what was now, once again, just a dark, distant fortress. It already felt as though he'd never set foot inside.

Ezra tensed; he saw something in his peripheral vision, or thought he did. Light poured through the sash window on the first floor of the mansion. He saw movement in the kitchen—it had to be them. It was now dark enough outside that he could potentially be seen, so he switched off the pool house lights and pulled a chair over to the sink to watch in secret.

A shadow moved behind the curtain in the kitchen of the mansion. He wished he could somehow get closer. An idea struck him. He grabbed his camera from the couch and rustled around in his pack until his fingers recognized the shape of his long-distance lens. He fit it to the mouth of the camera and sat back down and focused on the glowing window. With the lens, he was close enough to see a moth skittering about the far panels, trying to get at the source of light inside.

He zoomed back out to get a larger picture of the mansion and saw that two more windows were now lit up. His sight was obscured by the stained-glass patterns tracking up the tall stairway that composed the spine of the house. Distorted images, just smudges of darkness, circled up the staircase. They were almost to the third floor. The light to the master bedroom flicked on. The massive oriel window turned the dull yellow of drapes. He zoomed in. Nothing.

Then the drapes flung open. Hudson, jowls and cheeks peppered with a trim beard, tongue inside Sybil's mouth, one arm around her waist, and the other rubbing her crotch with fury. Sybil's left leg bent around him, blue slacks still fitted to her frame, but no shirt, only a black bra lilting at her sides. Then she was against the window, shifted, and the skin on her back bunched up beneath his groping paws. His gray slacks and black belt were loose.

Then Hudson turned Sybil around and put one hand on her hip and the other on her back and pushed her down onto her knees facing the outside world. She spread her fingers out wide on the windowpane and smudged the glass. Grant pulled down her pants, and with a fierce look on his face, began.

Ezra searched in vain for evidence on Sybil's face of anything other than pleasure. He held up the camera and smashed it and every picture inside on the floor.

FOURTEEN

Ezra chucked a handful of empty mini tequila bottles into a dense thicket of hawthorn outside Bryce's apartment building. A man with a leather jacket and slicked-back hair was on his way out, so Ezra didn't have to buzz in at the gate. The apartment building was three levels crowded around a pool. He'd once jumped from Bryce's second floor deck into the water on a dare. That seemed ages ago. That seemed a different jumper.

He circled the stairs up to the second floor walkway and past a few apartments. He stopped at Bryce's front door and gathered himself. He didn't hear anyone inside, but there was light on. He knocked.

No one answered.

He knocked again, and then texted *you home?*

Nothing.

He could picture Bryce in his bedroom, headphones on, engaged in some role-playing game, or maybe watching a porno, soundtrack bleating too loud into his eardrums to hear anything else. Ezra knew that in the planter box next to the door, beneath a neglected cherry tomato vine, rested a fake rock housing a key. He found it and pushed back the little metal slide. He failed to fit the key in the slot until he closed one eye and rubbed the teeth along the brass surface of the knob.

The living room was empty, but he heard the sound of a woman in the back, laughing, and the bassline to some 90s-era smooth funk piece. "Bryce?" he asked, loud, but there was no reply. "Bryce!" Nothing. He was about to walk back to the room when Bryce emerged. Shirt off, boxer shorts, sweating, Louisville Slugger raised.

"Ezra? How did you get in here?" He lowered the bat.

Ezra tossed the key and it landed on the carpet a few feet short. "I need to talk."

"Dude, you broke in?"

"Let myself in. There's some crazy shit happening."

Bryce blinked. "Uh, yeah, there *is* some crazy shit. Like what you did to April."

"I—"

"You slept with her and didn't call."

He felt his cheeks redden. But it felt odd. Since when had Bryce ever, in his entire life, said *slept with,* and not *screwed* or *boinked* or *fucked*? The voice in the other room—they weren't alone. And that wasn't Maria back there, either.

The music stopped. A head peeked around the corner, then a full body. It was April, with Bryce's faded Dodgers jersey hanging limp around her legs.

"It's not what you think," Bryce said.

"It's exactly what you think," April said.

Ezra just stood there.

"It's just that after you ditched her, one thing led to another—" Bryce said.

"Is that what this is?" April yelled. "One thing just *led* to another?"

"No," Bryce said. "Hold on. Let me think." He set down the bat and sank into a beige armchair, head in his hands.

She narrowed her eyes at Ezra. "What do you want?"

He didn't answer.

"Listen," Bryce said. "I need to figure some shit out."

"You think?" April said.

The shock wore off, and Ezra understood what had happened. In fact, it made perfect sense. As always, Bryce was being completely honest—one thing had led to another, and now here he was. April'd come knocking at his door to talk about what had happened, and he comforted her, and he'd become so caught up in it that Maria hadn't so much as entered his mind, and when she had, he just decided not to think about it, because that was something that he was able to do.

And now, faced with reality, in the form of Ezra, Bryce felt terrible—he really did—and hadn't a clue what to do to get out of it. But that was the thing with Bryce: he'd stop feeling terrible once he began concerning himself with something else.

For a moment, Ezra wondered if he was any different; he'd barely spared a thought for April over this past week. "April," he said. "I'm sorry. I apologize."

"You assholes deserve each other," she said. But as she tugged at her jersey and fingered the worn fabric, showing a bit of her beautiful shoulder, the look in her eyes surprised Ezra. She looked like she'd won a battle, here with Bryce on the couch, nearly fetal, ready to be manipulated into obedience.

Ezra backed toward the door and clasped his hands together. "Got it. Bryce? We'll talk later."

"Do you need a ride?" Bryce asked. The hopeful sap was already trying to escape.

April crossed her arms and rolled her eyes at Ezra, as if now—seconds after he'd apologized—they were already commiserating over the behavior of a teenage boy in need of discipline.

"I'm good." Ezra left. He walked down the steps without turning back. What hadn't he fucked up? Sybil was gone, and now, as a consolation prize, his best friend was shacked up with the only other girl he'd been intimate with since the afternoon his mother died.

Of all things, he didn't want to think about that, so he didn't, and somehow it worked. Maybe Bryce was rubbing off on him. He walked down the side street back on to the main drag. He passed the open windows of a hookah bar and breathed in the smell of incense. For a moment, he wondered about Maria, whether she knew about all of this. Probably not. Why else would Bryce be having a crisis in there? But soon she would know. Bryce would never tell her on his own, of course, but April would make him. Or if he resisted, she'd just tell Maria herself. She'd already revealed herself to Ezra.

Maria was probably at the hospital that very moment, tending to her patients, too caught up in the care of the sick and dying to spare a thought for what was happening at her fiancé's apartment with her good friend. Ezra felt a bit of anger at the injustice of it all. If anyone deserved more, it was her.

The whistle of airbrakes interrupted his thoughts. A bus pulled up next to him and a couple of teenagers hopped out. For the hell of it he got on and found a seat near the back, in front of a guy with dreadlocks. The bus hissed and began moving. Ezra watched the shop-lined city blocks pass, bright with neon. Pleather seat cushions stuck to his shirt. He was soaked from both drunken sweat and the miles he'd walked since first seeing Sybil and Grant in the window.

The bus slowed to a stop. On stepped a woman with hair dyed the color of snow. She was wrapped in dark stretchy work-out shorts that barely reached her thigh and a pink tank top of the same poly-something-fabric as her shorts. She strutted down the middle of the bus as if it were a catwalk, spun around, and sat across the aisle from Ezra.

She removed her sunglasses and began playing with her phone. Her features were loud, every one of them: skin pulled back from her eyes, skin pulled up from her forehead, pulled back by her jaw, giving everything a plastic sheen. Her eyebrows were absent save a few graphite swipes, nose carved from a bar of soap, lips off the dime shelf of a magic shop. In the faces of film industry beauties there was typically one dominant physical feature, maybe two, around which the rest of the more common facial traits were composed. This woman's face seemed ready to burst from all the amplification.

Ezra wondered whether anyone was ever really happy with their lot in life. He'd wondered this before, many times, probably been ordered to wonder it from the pulpit. But he was still drunk and the question seemed profound. Maybe his mother was right: everyone was blessed with deep caverns of need that nothing of this earth could fill, and that emptiness pushed them to do terrible things.

"What the fuck are you looking at?" the woman asked, head cocked sideways.

Ezra hadn't realized he'd been staring. He opened his mouth to apologize but was distracted by bright a facade outside. He saw a name in lights: *Sybil Harper*. He yanked on the wire hanging across the window. The driver pulled over and the bus jolted to a stop. Ezra stuffed a few dollars into the slot and the doors hissed open.

He rushed to the booth, paid, and found a seat in the back-left row of the theater. There weren't many people inside, and they were all spread out.

The lights went down. With each additional preview that passed, Ezra's insides began to fold and fold and fold until he felt like one tight, tiny, origami swan—these were all NC-17 flicks or straight-up pornos. It now made sense that everyone was spread out. The room was filled with people covered in hats and hoods.

Finally, the music cued and there she was, his love, that small, beautiful little knob in the center of her nose illuminated by a million tiny pixels. The shot panned out, showing her sunbathing on a lawn chair next to a large, Romanesque pool.

The next shot was the face of a guy wearing a T-shirt so tight it looked painted. He was watching her, hammer in hand, from the roof of the pool house.

Ezra laughed. A few people looked over, but who cared? It was as though this was all some kind of elaborate set-up. What if, without realizing it, this entire week Ezra had been part of a reality show starring Sybil Harper and Grant Hudson? There might be cameras recording him this very moment.

And this scene? He could see it now: a pool boy sleeping with Sybil Harper gets dumped by Sybil Harper and goes to see a movie about a pool boy who sleeps with Sybil Harper and then gets dumped by Sybil Harper.

God, this was rich. A part of him hoped he *was* being filmed. At least then the whole world would see how fucked up things really were. Would anyone bother to watch it? Of course! The real question was whether anyone would actually care.

The camera flipped to a shot inside the pool house. Sybil surprised the guy while he was changing his clothes, showing his impossibly carved abs.

"I've seen you watching," Sybil said to the silverback on screen. Her smooth chin dimpled and they began disrobing. The piano tinkling gave way to the string section, and then the horn section, until finally a pulsing bass and drumbeat flanked the orchestra as the couple fell to the ground in a perfectly managed pile of lust.

Ezra unzipped his pants, gritted his teeth, and went to work. He was furious. She'd made him into a piece of meat. She'd played him like the shitty part she was playing now on-screen. And all the things she'd told him! Wanting to be seen for who she really was? Understood? Not admired, but *loved*? No. He'd loved her, but not anymore. She would no longer be human to him. He'd make certain of it, right here and now.

He heard a rustling behind him and turned to find a flashlight glaring in his face.

"What the fuck, man?" A theater usher. The flashlight beam fell on Ezra's crotch.

Ezra jumped from his seat and pushed the usher to the ground. He ran up the aisle and out of the theater.

FIFTEEN

A replay of the NBA Finals from seasons before played in the dark on Ezra's television in the pool house and Grant Hudson didn't mind. He'd seen every minute of this game already from courtside seats, but change was afoot in real life, and when change was afoot he liked his television how he liked his employees: with no surprises.

Until tonight, he would have said he preferred his wife this way too, and Sybil had always complied. But now he found it refreshing that she'd finally stepped out. Here he was, alone in the pool house, watching his gardener's television, 9mm pistol loaded and resting on his midseam, waiting for the fun to start.

The filming over the last week or so in Vancouver had been a metaphor for his life of late. Half of the crew was new and insecure, so Grant had been forced to make more decisions than usual, ones far below his pay grade. Explaining things that people already knew but were too scared to take responsibility for? Tedium. It didn't used to be like this. Early in his career—before the successes—he had to fight his staff in order to get them to do what he said.

If only he'd have known at the time how much more fun that was. But could he really blame it on the staff? Were they not just nerve endings of a greater system? Sure, he'd become too powerful for his position. But the real problem was this: there was so little *juice*. Sure, there were tens, sometimes hundreds of millions on the line, but even that had become commonplace. And after so many years of trying to pry wallets open, the public finally trusted him and his taste, so the people who had money to spend on such things trusted him as well. The wallets were his and success was predictable.

Blah, blah, blah yes he *had* taken that one loss with that romantic comedy a few years back, and yes, he *should* have known better. The audience for adolescent romantic comedies had easily the lowest IQ of all moviegoers, so was it his fault for assuming he could be smart enough to be dumb enough to please the offspring of dunces?

He was his only competition, and anyone with an IQ above romcom knew that trying to defeat yourself was self-defeating. If the question driving one's creative life was *Can I summon enough energy to care about making this a success?* then a larger failure was already occurring.

So yes, it was shameful to admit, but a few years back that larger failure had led him to ask the natural questions regarding existence. He'd visited a famous spiritualist and flipped tarot cards and watched a sunset or two and come to the conclusion that the natural course of his life would be to turn to politics. Nowhere were the stakes higher. Just thinking about lofty, centuries-old words like *gubernatorial* summoned a fearful taste of copper to the back of his tongue.

But there'd been so much waiting. Long red lights and short yellow lights but no fucking green. Nowhere but in politics was the powerbase so cautious, nepotistic, bureaucratic, myopic, -ic, -ic, -ic. So here he was, in the plebe Ezra Fog's living room, drinking shitty beer and watching reruns while waiting for a chance to do something significant enough to get the blood flowing to areas other than his organs for continuation of life and his bowels for daily constitutionals.

A test. A rite of passage. Just like the old days, before everything went south, those times as a youngster when he'd failed at some sort of knucklehead prank, or been caught skipping school, and his father would pick up the .22 and count to ten, and by the time he was halfway up the hill to the forest, little plugs would be thumping into the soil behind his shoes. If you survived the night, you could consider yourself forgiven.

The television froze and morphed for a moment, then unfroze and once again the seconds wound down in the fourth quarter of the game, a quarter that he remembered perfectly— his curse—as being peppered with time-outs. He took another sip of beer but was interrupted by a crunching sound out of the side window, which he'd left open. He flipped off the television and laid there in the dark, pawing the pistol back and forth, the metal warm and damp from his hands.

A key jiggled against the lock, once, twice, and again. He figured the kid must be drunk.

The door opened and a shadow entered. It stumbled around, keys jangling, and didn't even bother turning on the lights. Ezra. Grant realized he hadn't thought much about him, specifically. He'd more been mulling over what Sybil's affair would mean for his marriage and future in the movie business and politics. But now with Ezra here in the flesh, he felt anger—not much, just a prick—but anger, nonetheless. And not because Ezra had fucked Sybil—the picture of them in his mind caused no more disdain than a stage test with poor cinematography—but what the affair represented: disrespect.

Anyone in an affair with a touchy-feely like Sybil knew that few fucks were more vigorous than those that involved a bit of deception. Sybil cared about Grant enough to hate him, so that abundance of anger and angst was surely poured into the exchange with Ezra, the adulteress hollering subtext through the romp: *See? My husband has no right to take me for granted. He must be crazy for treating me this way when I can be this . . . damn . . . good.* It had to have been epic. Hadn't he put Sybil through all those years of crap?

One of the things Grant appreciated most about Sybil was her gift for suffering. She enjoyed it. She was a natural. Her empathy and overactive conscience made it nearly impossible for her to resist entertaining pain when it presented itself, which was why they'd worked so well together for so long.

But for her to disrespect him? No. Hell no. Especially not when she'd done so with this failure of a man now stumbling around in the dark in front of him.

Grant cleared his throat.

Ezra froze next the couch. "Who's there?"

There was fuzz in the words; yes, Ezra was drunk. "Mr. Fog, good to see you. Hope you are well, etcetera, etcetera. I'm back and ready to collect some pictures of my wife in the midst of lewd behavior with unsatisfying men."

Ezra flipped on the lights.

From his horizontal position on the couch Grant leveled his pistol at Ezra's crotch. Ezra's face was flush with sweat, blotchy. It occurred to Grant that on a less attractive person, Ezra's look might have been awful, but on him it looked somewhat tragic, borderline sophisticated. If he ever showed up strung out at any of the coffee shops near the studios, he'd likely land a part or two, or at least work as a high-paid male escort.

Grant switched the gun to his other hand and sighted up the spot from Ezra's crotch to a place just above his heart. "I'm kidding, of course, about our little deal. But I do wish that you'd taken me up on my offer instead of, well, using it as inspiration. Anyhow, I nodded off twice before you finally returned. For a moment, I wondered if we'd lost you."

Ezra looked around, clearly unable to discern what Grant meant by *we*.

"Oh, Sybil isn't here, but she told me to tell you that she appreciated your services."

Ezra glanced at the gun.

"Oh no, she's fine, kiddo," said Grant. "Sleeping soundly. And not in the metaphorical sense. No cement shoes. I mean she's asleep up in our room. Perhaps snoring like a wildebeest if she's on her back—but you probably know all about that."

"Go fuck yourself."

Grant watched as the bones in Ezra's jaw pressed the skin out from his cheeks like little knuckles. The expression was a little exaggerated, but not bad. At the very least soap opera material.

"What do you want?" Ezra asked.

Grant felt more anger. Lovely. He'd been expecting a bleating calf, cowering before the butcher. He took a deep breath and crossed his legs. The longer one paused after a direct, emotional question, the more insecurity and doubt had a chance to enter the accused's mind. "Oh, before I forget. I wanted to tell you: while up in Vancouver I did a little research on hummingbird behavior. I discovered that they are incredibly territorial. I found pictures of male hummingbirds with wings broken, beaks. Vicious creatures, really." Hudson grunted as he swung his feet around to the floor. "You look terrible. Hangover?"

Ezra said nothing.

"Ah, still pleasantly drunk. Anyhow, we'll have more time to chat in the car. Your car." Hudson flipped his pistol in the direction of the door.

Ezra paused and again looked at the gun. Grant noticed his hands flexing. "Where are we going?"

Grant racked the slide of the pistol, chambering a round.

Ezra stared him down before walking out the door. Grant followed in silence. Oh dear, the nubile gardener reeked of tequila. It was amazing what you could tell about people from what they allowed themselves to smell like. Every deodorant had its connotations, every perfume its social class, but no one paid close enough attention. In this techno-America, the leading roles were the eyes and the ears, and the rest of the senses served as extras.

He took a deep sniff. Yes, tequila, and bottom shelf at that. You could trust a tequila drinker. Everyone was false in their own way, but tequila drinkers were like rum drinkers: the only people they meant to harm were themselves. Not like whiskey and bourbon drinkers, who all had something to prove. But gin drinkers? Masters of artifice, never to be trusted. He loved the smell of juniper.

The gravel on the side of the pool house crunched beneath their feet. It made sense that Sybil would go for a tequila drinker. She probably worshipped the tastes of this workingman. A boy with calloused hands! Was dumpster diving, for someone in Sybil's place, not the ultimate in condescension? To screw the cabana boy? People called Grant arrogant, but then again, people tended to stay—at all costs—in the exact same social class in which they were raised. Grant considered one of his biggest advantages to be this: having spent decades on both ends of the socioeconomic spectrum, he never assumed someone's class gave them any inferiority or superiority, blind ignorance or esoteric intelligence.

Whittled down, the truth was this: The rich and the poor viewed each other with awe and terror and anger and pity and jealousy and disdain. They foisted on each other every yearning that a human could feel. They imagined in each other a god: unknowable, cloaked in mystery. In short, both the rich and poor thought they were different, when in fact, they were the same.

Ezra was still a man, no matter how feeble, and deserved to be treated as such. Revenge, when personal, could be a show of respect.

They stopped at Ezra's sedan.

"Tinted windows," said Grant. "Convenient. Get in front. Let's pretend this is a rideshare service. Meanwhile, I'll stay in the back with the gun. Got any bottled water?"

"Fuck off." Ezra clicked the electronic lock opening the doors.

"Oh, and before you get in, please lend me your phone."

Ezra tossed it onto the back seat and they both climbed in. Ezra's sedan smelled like clipped grass. There were a handful of

empty coffee cups lying on the seat and in the footwells alongside stray jumper cables missing their case.

"Where are we going?" Ezra asked.

"The beach! I don't care what route you take. Just don't get
pulled over. If you do, well, then we'll get creative. I'll let you
ponder what that might entail."

Hudson could see in the rearview mirror that Ezra's eyes
had narrowed.

"Ooh, that glare. Icy. Well, I've never been a big fan of them
either . . . unintended consequences, I mean." Hudson rubbed
his palms together and rolled down the window a tad. It was
getting muggy inside, probably from Ezra sweating out the
cheap tequila. "You're fit to drive, right?"

Ezra opened his mouth to speak.

"Just kidding. Of course you are." He tapped the nozzle
of the pistol against the side of Ezra's head. "Firearms sober a
person up far better than black coffee." Grant leaned back into
the seat. "Now calm down. I'm not going to shoot you just
yet."

The car backed out of the driveway. Grant for a moment
felt like a little kid. How long since he'd been in the rear seat,
except for the limos studio heads rented for red carpet events?
Was it with his father, that bourbon drinker, that soft shell of
a man who worked at a canning factory and stank of cod?
Who proved his worth by bruising walls, doors, bumpers, bank
accounts, and most of all, flesh, if not that of his peers, then that
of his wife and son?

Grant could remember it like yesterday, the back of his par-
ent's car, dry summer dust making him cough, passing a stretch
of sandy beach built by a small river emptying into an inlet,

where a twenty-odd foot sailboat, navy blue with a battered ash hull, was resting on its side, beached.

Yes. Like yesterday. They were on the way to meet his destiny at the courthouse. At this time, he still went by his given name: Frederick Chance.

The elder Grant Hudson—his namesake—came to town in a late-sixties Buick model that their streets had never seen, talking about plans for a highway junction and, after that, a shipping port that would service every town on the tip of the northeastern coastline. He was a developer. He had detailed sketches of the building plans. He used words like *infrastructure* and knew the yearly catch numbers and projections better than the cannery managers themselves did. He had certified letters from a senator. He was a first-rate con artist, so of course he wanted substantial investments up front. And he wanted the brunette with the high cheekbones and soft eyes: Frederick Chance's mother.

Frederick didn't know why he and his father were on their way to see Grant Hudson, except for the fact that his mother had not been home the night before. Apparently, she needed to think something through, but *not to worry*—his father had relayed this information a dozen times the night before as both of them sat by the fireplace, tobacco smoke hanging in the air, dogs digging through soil in their sleep.

As Ezra drove, the memory continued in Grant's mind. He and his father passed the beach and continued west up the hill, past clusters of houses to city hall, which was really just another building on the block of storefronts. But with the help of the elder Grant Hudson, it soon promised to have white Roman pillars and an enormous clock tower with a bell that would announce the hours with such force that fisherman miles off-shore would have no need for timepieces.

Frederick's father parked on the other side of the street from the brown building. "Stay here," he said, and got out.

"But—"

His father slammed the door in response, and Frederick stayed put. He knew better than to disagree. Arguing and disobedience were the same thing in his family, and both typically ended in violence. He had scars and bruises to prove it. Too many to count. He'd brag about them to his friends at school whenever they'd compare injuries. Once, his father had cold-cocked him with a milk bottle and he'd felt dizzy for over a week. It was frustrating, because there was no way to prove to his friends that the injury had actually happened.

But as Frederick Chance watched his father pull his news-boy cap low and shove his hands into the front pockets of his trousers and walk, hunched over, across the street, something occurred to him that never had before. That walk: there was something about it, something that was there the whole time but needed the gravity of this moment to reveal. His father always walked as though it was freezing outside. His father walked as though bracing for a blow.

Across the street, waiting, was Hudson. He wore a gray, double-breasted suit, remarkable for its color. It wasn't the dark gray of a raincloud, like the one suit all of the men in town owned, if they owned any at all. Hudson's was the light gray of a cresting wave. Had any man in town worn it, he would have been mocked until someone got drunk enough to challenge him to a fight. Traveling salesmen always dressed down when visiting—denim and flannel—to better connect with the townspeople. But Grant Hudson seemed to have no desire to pretend he wasn't better than everyone else.

As Frederick Chance watched, he knew he should scoff, as surely his father would, as would everyone else he knew. But he couldn't. There was something different about this man. Something bold and audacious and demanding of respect. He came in as a lord, with a white Detroit stallion. A man who knew that these people weren't looking for someone like them. They weren't even looking for someone to emulate. They were looking for someone they could never be.

Frederick's father stopped at the steps of city hall and began talking to Grant Hudson. By their body language, it was clearly more than a simple greeting. Where was his mother? What did this rich guy have to do with them? Hudson gestured to his magnificent car parked alongside the building. His father, hands still in his pockets, kicked at the curb, as if trying to dislodge something. He took off his cap and scratched his scalp. He folded the brim in his hands. He coughed into his fist. Every move betrayed weakness.

Then Frederick's father nodded, turned around, and walked back to the car. He opened the door but wouldn't meet his son's eyes. "Go talk to him."

"Where's Mom?"

"Go." He couldn't read his father at the time, but what he saw in his memory was the most precise look of human shame he would ever see.

Frederick got out of the car and stopped.

"Go!" His father shoved him out into the road. Hudson loomed, arms crossed, light gray fedora shading a scowl.

Frederick walked up, the whole way conscious of his hands and what to do with them. He stopped short. Grant Hudson would scarcely look at him.

"You can come with us," Hudson said, as much to the other side of the street as he did to Frederick. Finally, he looked straight at him. His eyes were piercing. "I'd rather you stayed here, but I promised your mother, and I keep my promises."

"I—"

"She's in the car. Go speak to her and make your decision. Don't let anyone make it for you."

As he walked up to Hudson's car, his hands tingled. Inside sat his mother, in a hat he'd never seen before, one of those adorned with flowers and beads and a brim askew like that boat on the shore. She smiled, and her lip trembled, and he understood.

Years later, when he thought about it, he guessed that she'd been on the edge for a long time. Trapped with a man who didn't feel trapped. A man she respected but could not understand. A man who punished her and their child rather than face his own demons. She'd married the mystery of him, only to find the mystery was simply desire sucked dry by regret and hopelessness. So, there she sat, in the magnificent car of Grant Hudson.

"What's going on?" Frederick asked.

She paused, and put her finger to her nose for a moment. "I am leaving your father. Mr. Hudson has agreed that you can come with us."

Agreed. Not hoped. "I don't understand."

"I'd be okay with you coming along," she said, and then glanced past him. Frederick turned and saw Grant Hudson watching from the street.

Something inside him burst. He felt an anger he'd never felt before. He didn't have words for it yet, but he understood. This deal had already been made. The choice was his, but in reality, he was a risk she hoped she wouldn't have to take.

Frederick stifled his tears.

His mother looked straight ahead. "He's waiting on your decision."

So cold. So very cold. Later, he understood—all too well—but God did he hate her in that moment. He felt like spitting in her face through the window of that pretentious car. Instead, he turned on his heels and ran past Hudson, straight to his father, and buried his face into his trousers. He felt a hand on his forehead for a moment, and then nothing. He squatted on the ground and cried. Finally, he caught his breath. When he turned around, Grant Hudson's car—and his mother—were gone.

"That was a stupid decision you made," his father said.

Frederick balled his fists, fingernails digging into his palm, but didn't say anything. His father had a dazed look, one he would continue to develop, as if his eyes had turned inward. A look that would stay on his face even after he died, from a heart attack, less than two years later.

Ezra's sedan proceeded slowly up the city's artery, along the arm of the coast, and the memory of his father's death made Grant realize that he'd forgotten to take his blood pressure pills. It'd have to wait until he got back.

But fuck it. By God, what a night! He took a tin of cherry chew from his back pocket and popped a pinch into his lower lip. He rarely chewed anymore but this was vacation, baby. He laid his right hand across the back of the seat.

Ezra peered through the rearview mirror.

"Want a dip?" Hudson asked.

Ezra didn't respond. Grant noticed that his hands were at ten and two on the wheel. Who drove like that? "Yeah, you're not the type," Grant rolled down the window and spit. "You grew up stuffing nihilistic moaners into your DVD player and flipping through highbrow books you didn't understand in hopes they'd give you the cultural currency you couldn't create on your own. You took deep drags on unfiltered cigarettes and had trouble keeping your bangs out of your eyes and ended your sentences with *man*. I made serious money from terrible films because your type conflates confusion with depth."

"You don't know shit about me."

"You sure about that?" They stopped at a red light and a slim guy with a severely undercut flop of hair, walking barefoot in ripped highwater jeans held in place by enormous brass belt buckle, plus a western shirt and a bowtie, crossed the street. "I bet that outfit *means* something."

Ezra remained silent.

"C'mon! I know, I know, I have a gun, and I fucked up your tryst, but at least humor me by engaging in some conversation. I'm bored." Grant chuckled and patted him on the shoulder. Finally, he could smell on Ezra, along with the tequila, the faintest pinesap whiff of fear.

Ezra said nothing.

"Seriously though. Do you know what I read for kicks? Celebrity memoirs. The ones that moralize about how to get ahead in life by describing their author's own rise. You've got to agree, there's nothing funnier than hearing a rich person try to explain how they got their money and then justify why they still have it."

Ezra looked out the window and wiped something from his ear. "So what?"

"What do you mean, *so what*?"

"You have a gun to my head and you're telling me about celebrity memoirs. I could give a shit what people do with their money and why."

"Am I getting a rise out of you?"

Ezra rolled his shoulders.

"Listen up," Grant said. "Every rich person, without fail, tries to pass the buck. Whether it be to God, principles, luck, or victimhood, no one really wants to admit that their wealth is theirs because they're choosing to hoard it. It's so much more convenient to believe you've been chosen, so much easier to justify keeping the money if you've been deemed special by something beyond you and your coughing and shitting and pissing and body odor."

Ezra said nothing.

"Your body odor, by the way," said Grant, "is cheap tequila and fear."

"What about philanthropists? Taking care of your family?"

"Philanthropists fly jets, Ezra. Philanthropists sway elections. Philanthropists give money because they fear villagers, pitchforks, and ultimately, the guillotine. And families? Ever stop to think about which families consistently hold positions of power in both public and private? Ever research the bloodlines of the elite?"

"You should write a celebrity memoir."

"So should you. *One Week with Sybil!* It might sell a few dozen copies." Grant spit out the window again. He could smell something rotting, along with the ocean. "I'm waiting," he continued, "for the day someone writes a memoir and never even implies a word about deserving or not deserving anything. That'll be a worthwhile read. Are you curious why? Of course you are, you have a gun to your head! Well, first, I've never met another rich person who is comfortable, deep down, with being rich. Half the reason all these tycoons have houses and yachts so big they need staffs is so they can justify paying people to be around them all the time. They can't stand to be alone with their guilt."

". . . and your residence is so modest?"

"Not compared to yours. But your residence isn't exactly modest, either, compared to, well, probably 98 percent of the world. But who's counting? Oh, right. All of us—but we only count those who have more than we do. Otherwise we might feel guilty. And we might actually have to reflect on who we are, instead of all the ingenious methods we've found of avoiding the truth.

"But to your question: why do I live on such palatial grounds? I'm just keeping up appearances, keeping the trust of these insecure trust funders. There's a reason you haven't seen me much. I prefer my solitude."

Through the rearview mirror, Grant saw Ezra roll his eyes.

"Hah! I am getting a rise out of you."

"Hardly," Ezra said.

"That's fine, repress it. Let it grow in the loamy soil of your subconscious. Soon it will bloom and become a memoir. See, I don't feel the need to apologize for my wealth. This points to the fundamental difference between that barefoot spaz with the bowtie and myself. I have no need to make a statement, no need for anyone to understand me. I have no need to share my humanity with anyone."

"That's funny, because you can't seem to stop talking about yourself."

"Touché! But ah, this isn't sharing, Ezra. This my gift to you. A lesson—granted, it's being given to a man who most likely won't be around to spread it. But sharing is the last thing I want, because our shared humanity really just means our shared weakness. And once a weakness is revealed, it's basically an invitation. *Come take what I have!*" Grant spit out the window.

They passed a party of some sort that was just getting started at a residence up the hill from the roadside. There were the usual security guards on the street, a few catering trucks, and a lineup of vehicles.

They veered right and cruised down a grade, past a long flat beach flanked by a few bulldozers, each waiting for daylight so they might push around sand, and then further along to a cove named after a vaudeville actor who'd long since passed. The ocean roared, and the smell of the salt water hit Grant's nose.

That smell often brought up sentimental feelings from Grant's childhood on the other coast, but they rarely conjured memories, so this was an exception. As they drove, he remembered a warm Friday night near the end of September on the North Atlantic Coast when he was twelve.

He'd been busy doing his homework at the dinner table, fire popping, a plate of pork loin, mashed potatoes, and seared carrots grown cold on the table, when the front door slammed open.

His father stepped in and scanned the room. "Where is she?"

His mother was out back, coaxing the hens into the hen-house for the night. Frederick hopped from his seat and made for his father. He immediately recognized the violence in his voice and knew the best way to negotiate such situations. "Can I get you a drink?"

His father pushed him into the wall, still looking around. "Don't patronize me," he said, breath stinking of yeast and onions. "Where is she? And don't you dare lie."

"Mom's out back, putting in the hens. Been here all night. Don't worry, I'll go get her."

His father paused and glared at him through his glassy eyes, one of them puffy and turning purple. He'd been in a fight already.

"She's just outside," Frederick continued. "Here, let me take your coat."

He reached for it but his father slapped his hand. "I'll deal with my own damn coat. What are you, a fucking maid? Go get her."

Frederick hustled out to the back and found his mother closing the door to the henhouse. Theirs was a beautiful property, bordered by coastal spruce, with a small feeder creek running through its center. "Mom!"

"Yes, darling."

"Dad's home." He hoped that the sound of his voice would be enough to let her know the situation.

She paused for a moment, and with her foot nudged the last of the Rhode Island Reds into the coop.

"He was calling for you."

"Did you fix him a drink?"

"I tried."

She closed the door to the henhouse tight.

"We could tell him one of the hens got out," Frederick said, "and you'd gone chasing her." He glanced over his shoulder.

She tousled his hair, sighed, and walked back toward the house, swinging her coat over her shoulders, as if bored.

He followed.

Later, Frederick discovered the issue. His mother had purchased an emerald-green, boatneck swing dress after the lobster season, and worn it to a fund-raiser at town hall where most everyone was gathered to mingle and celebrate the end of summer and the start of a new school year. Frederick had witnessed his father's swoons when he saw her twirl in the living room. But a few nights later, after a few drinks, some of the cannery boys began talking about that dress, and Frederick's father took exception. On the way home, he began to question his wife's motives for buying such a dress.

Frederick followed his mother inside from the henhouse. He did his best to stand between them, and took as many licks as he was able to, but in the end, he was knocked unconscious. His mother didn't get out of bed the next morning, and neither did his father. They never talked about it, and she never wore a dress again.

Grant snapped out of the memory and realized that they were now miles up the coastline. "What was I saying?" he asked.

"I don't remember."

No matter. No reason to think about such things, not any longer. Both were now dead and the tobacco was spicy on his tongue. A bit of ocean mist floated by the lights illuminating the empty byways. A coffee shop. A lone grocery store. Surf rentals. Tacos. They were in the capillaries of the city now, and very little blood was flowing. "Do you believe in tests, Ezra?"

"What do you mean?"

"It's a simple question."

"I guess it depends on the test."

"Well, I'm a big believer. People get caught up in what is being tested and whether or not a particular test works a certain way, etcetera. But all tests show results, even if what they show is unintended."

"Am I being tested right now?"

Hudson closed his eyes and laughed, shaking his head. "He asks and yet he's a gardener."

"Groundskeeper. And so what?"

"One moment. About that. Something's been bothering me. What exactly is a literate, attractive, white American male doing in that job?"

"Ask your wife," Ezra said.

"Ah, I forgot. You guys must have really connected. Shared your feelings. Had meaningful conversations. But Ezra, come on, buddy! I know that you've been in that job for years. And regardless, of course you're being tested. How about I put it into terms you'll better understand."

They drove up a slope and down, then past a beach and a seafood joint resting merely yards past the county line—the tip of a fingernail stretched just beyond the edge of the reaching arms of the city.

"You plant three shrubs," Grant continued. "One thrives. Needs to be constantly trimmed so it doesn't take over space it wasn't intended to occupy. The second does just *okay*. It survives but isn't at risk of endangering any of its neighbors. The third, well, you wonder whether it will outlast winter, even with the pains you've taken to ensure its success. Yet, despite all this, in the end, it's the gardener who has the power to decide who lives and who dies."

"So you're the gardener," said Ezra.

"Groundskeeper," said Grant. "And no, my friend, we're all shrubs. I'm just trying to find out how you grow."

"And how do *you* grow?"

"I'll give you one guess," Grant said. There was no one else on the road, and they were almost there.

SIXTEEN

The left is just past the next mile marker," Hudson said from the back seat. "Now, Ezra, here's where the shrub metaphor breaks down—"

Shut. The. Fuck. Up, Ezra thought. He looked in the rearview and imagined how Hudson might look robed before a podium, no different than the traveling preachers he'd seen, trying to prove—to use Grant's words—how special *they* were to the rest of the world. The skin on his hand was hot from gripping the steering wheel. He wanted to pummel the guy.

"—sometimes, if you stop watering that third shrub, starve it of nutrients, even put a sack over it so it gets not the slightest bit of sun, when you finally return it to the conditions it squandered, the shrub will not just thrive, but dominate everything near it." Grant cleared a nostril into his palm.

Ezra's mother would have had a field day breaking apart Hudson's simplistic justifications for how he operated in the world. He knew he needed to keep calm, but he couldn't resist muttering, "Brave new theories of landscape management."

Hudson laughed. "That's the spirit! You may yet make it through the night. Now take a left at that wooden post."

Ezra slowed the car and turned onto a dirt road weaving between thick walls of bramble and down a steep embankment to the shore. Each switchback was only just wide enough for his car. He couldn't see further ahead than a few yards. His headlights illuminated something solid, not a gate but more of a nondescript black wall, perhaps metal, with no markings whatsoever. The moment Ezra stopped the car, the wall began to slide open.

"Veer left," Hudson said.

Ezra drove on. Past the wall, both roads were paved with asphalt, and Ezra could make out a large building down to the right. He lost view of it as once again a cave of brambles swallowed them.

"Summer home?" Ezra asked.

"It's always summer."

The car emerged from the bramble. The asphalt gave way to a geometric smattering of gray and brown stone pieces, reminiscent of the patio back at the mansion. His mind flashed for a moment to Hudson making love to Sybil. He quickly dismissed it.

"Park anywhere," said Hudson.

Ezra pulled up against a wooden rail dividing the property from the beach, got out, and shut the door. The anger he felt toward Hudson ebbed into a dull fear. He tried to get a sense of the place, but couldn't see much in the way of lights either up or down the beach, just a dim glow from what looked like a deck seventy-five feet up the hill behind them. The rest was cliff rock and scraggle giving way to shadowy swales of sand, peppered with beach grass shifting in the light wind.

"I own the rest of the lots on this stretch of beach."

Ezra nodded. Meaning *no one can see us.* Meaning *don't think you're going to just scream, or duck away.* A brief wave of anxiety flooded through Ezra, but what he felt surging through his fingers and neck wasn't a panic attack. This was no condition, no disorder. It was honest fear. Ezra took a few deep breaths and tamped down the feelings. Slowly he left his body and felt himself standing beside himself, as if he were a physician, taking notes, as if the fear was happening to a different body altogether. If nothing else, he'd had practice at this sort of thing. A steady calm returned.

Hudson pointed his pistol out past the railing toward the ocean. "Go on."

"What are we doing?" But suddenly he knew. The ocean for the pool boy. A gust of wind rippled Ezra's T-shirt. The air smelled the sweet of rotting seaweed.

"Haven't you guessed?"

"You're going to see what kind of shrub I am."

"Smart man." Grant pointed to a boat, small and plastic and shaped like a rectangle, lying upside down in dune grass. It didn't look as though it had been used in quite some time. "Pull it out to the tide line."

The dinghy was perhaps twelve feet long and looked like the bottom half of a sedan, without the wheels. Stable, but probably at the cost of grace. Ezra dragged it by the bow along the sand toward where he could hear small waves breaking. Everything took on a larger presence. The sand sinking below his sneakers was real. The gun in Hudson's palm. This shitty boat.

"The bay is sheltered from the swell," said Hudson. "But I'm sure we'll still manage to get a little wet."

They reached the tide line. White water scuttled in. Hudson slipped off his brown loafers and Ezra removed his sneakers.

Hudson gestured slightly with the pistol. "Do me a favor and wade out a bit. Get the boat to where it's just floating."

The water rushed around his feet and seeped up the legs of his jeans. It was cool but not cold. Now those elaborate justifications Hudson had made on the ride over were more terrifying than absurd. Hudson was the worst kind of crazy: calculating. This was no crime of passion. This was fun. This was a stage.

Ezra pulled the boat out into the whitewash of the small waves until it became buoyant in his hands.

Hudson grabbed hold of the boat's boxy stern. An airplane flying overhead buzzed. In his mind, for a brief moment, Ezra was brought back to the bedroom with Sybil, gazing out the window at vapor trails. Where was she now? Sleeping? He hoped so.

"You get in first," said Hudson. "I'll hold."

Ezra climbed in. Just as he got situated in the bow, Hudson gave the boat a push further into the water and hopped in himself, showing athleticism not apparent in his build. The boat jockeyed beneath them, and the waves, though small, were beginning to push them sideways and back toward shore. Hudson retrieved two small aluminum-and-plastic oars from one side of the boat and slid them over. "Stuff the rings in the oar locks," he said. "Then start rowing."

After a few feeble attempts, Ezra managed, one small gush at a time, to propel the boat in the direction of the open ocean. Every so often a wave crested over the lip of the bow and sprayed his back, but soon he only felt slight rises and falls. The roar of breaking water retreated to a faint rush.

Hudson coughed lightly into his fist. With his pointer finger he dug out the tobacco from his lip and flicked it over the side.

"So, what sort of game are we playing?" Ezra asked. He imagined the depth of the water beneath him, how much would fill in over his head were his feet to touch bottom.

"No games. This is just a balancing of the scales."

"Adultery weighs the same as murder?"

"Who said anything about murder?"

Ezra rowed. Grant was looking out to the left at something, palming the pistol on his knee. He didn't look like a famous movie producer, here in this small boat, with his shorts and stocky legs and bare feet. He looked like a suburban retiree, a snowbird from Arizona, fresh from the golf course. But his shoulders were broad. If it came to a fight, he might be difficult to take down. Ezra's thoughts were interrupted by a scratching beneath the boat. Shark? He glanced to the side and could make out the shape of orb clusters on the surface in the dim light. Kelp heads. He wondered how many of them it would take to keep someone afloat. He could still hear the fuzz of waves breaking on shore. The lights on the property blinked over Hudson's shoulder.

"Beautiful night," Hudson said.

"Remind me again what we're doing."

"So very impatient. Fine, let's have some fun. I'll let you take a guess, for being such a good chauffer and for doing such a fine job with the grounds. And I'll make it easier on you if you're right."

"You're going to make me swim for it."

Grant laughed. "Good! But that was too easy. Only worth half a mile."

Ezra was in good shape, but yard work wasn't swimming. "How many miles are we talking about here?"

"Up to you." Hudson stared at him. "Once again, I have to ask the question, because it's out there. Why are you a gardener?"

"The same reason you're a movie producer."

"Enlighten me."

Ezra paused, took a stroke back out, and shrugged. All of a sudden, this all felt funny. It occurred to Ezra that he had an advantage here, and the advantage was this: Hudson already thought he knew him. If this was a game, he might as well play it. "To spite my parents."

In the dark, Ezra imagined Hudson's eyes flinching. Had he hit a target? This was the first crack he'd seen. Then Grant smiled, chuckled, and was back to his usual self. "Paging Dr. Freud. Where's your trim little tennis beard?"

"It's back with my Birkenstocks."

"I can see the tan lines on your feet. But yes, parents. Who gave them the right to bring you and me into the world? We certainly didn't ask for it."

Ezra shrugged. "Why does a shrub produce pollen and seeds?"

"Why, indeed. And now I understand more why you haven't done anything with your life. Being nothing has preserved your dream of being special. If you're not misunderstood, miscast, the victim of your own tragedy, then what are you? Conventional. Which is, to you, unacceptable—"

Ezra said nothing, just did his best to appear as though he was listening. But trying *not* to be conventional? Please. Conventional was what he'd wished he could be his entire life: the norm by which everyone else judged themselves as different. That way, no one would ever question whether he belonged, and he could finally feel free to be the same on the outside as he was on the inside. But now? With Hudson holding forth with a gun in his hand, in the process of executing some elaborate form of revenge? All of that business about *belonging* seemed precious, if not absurd. The tanned grasses on the property he kept were starved for water, not fertilizer.

He needed to survive. So, as Hudson held forth, he shifted his grip on the oars, so that they were now slicing through the water a bit sideways instead of pressing full against the current.

"—your parents, your teachers, and everyone else insisted you were special. You were made to understand this, but at some point you realized that, in fact, you were not. Decent looks, decent smarts, decent talent—nothing more. But— and here's the kicker, Ezra, hold on to your seat—rather than accepting that everyone around you was wrong about you, rather than embracing your lot in life, you realized a different way you could be special. You might not have had what it took to become famous on your own merit, but you could enjoy the infamy of victimhood."

Grant stopped and let that sit for effect. Ezra took a few full strokes so as not to tip Grant off to what he was doing with the oars, as they'd slowed down dramatically.

"No, not victims," Grant said. "What do they call them now? Ah yes. *Survivors*. You might not have had what it takes to go on your own quest, but you could survive someone else's. All you needed was a victimizer, and lo-and-behold, one appeared, then another, and another, and you took what they had to offer and waited. But then something even more terrible happened.

Gasp! You realized that your victimhood relative to others was also conventional. You were a survivor of only garden-variety misdeeds—pardon the pun—by minor villains. So, you began taking risks. Trying to lure a big fish in to tear you apart and make you famous. Eventually, you arrived here, in the land of big fish, to play the most obvious of roles: the pool boy. Congratulations. Here I am. Your shark."

"Funny," Ezra said. "I was always under the impression that I'd come here to escape my past."

"The greatest con artist is one's own mind."

Ezra pretended to let that all sink in. But at the same time, he found that it was, in fact, sinking in. Sure, with his life at hazard, this all seemed absurd, but what about the years—hell, the decade—that he'd spent waiting? And for what?

"This should do," Hudson said. "I can tell you're thinking—"

A swell rolled beneath them; above coughed a jetliner banking into an airport. Other than that, the only action was tiny waves lapping against the boat.

"—and now, Ezra, you at least begin to see my reasoning. If you were a bigger fish, maybe I'd just bury you."

"You have experience with that?"

"This in particular? You ask because you want more proof from me that you are special. You're like Sybil—"

Ezra wished he'd kept his mouth shut. A few more misplaced words and Grant might just make it ten miles.

"—she has this effect on people, you've realized," Grant said. "Making them believe they are the only ones in the world that matter. That quality made her rich. That quality made you her boy." Grant took the pistol, uncocked it, and stuffed it into the holster on his lower back. "But no, Ezra, I'm not going to shoot you. I'm going to let you prove my point.

"You see, as I was watching television in your living room I made a little bet with myself. I gave it 80/20 that once we got out here, if I had a pistol loaded and cocked, you would jump out of the boat without a fuss. You would once again confirm your role of victim, trajectory unchanged. But those odds were boring. It would be too easy. So instead, I decided to make it 60/40 by holstering the gun. One of us will have to swim to shore. The other will row. And now, as they say, *it's your move*." He patted his hands on his knees and watched.

"So, what, we're supposed to fight?" Ezra wished that rage he'd felt in the car, when taking down Grant felt like just a matter of letting his feelings escape, was still inside of him.

"Up to you. Or you could just jump out and swim."

They both stayed still for a moment, silent. Ezra kept waiting for something to happen. But it didn't. His hands were starting to shake. "This is ridiculous."

Grant started laughing. "You don't know what to do, do you? Or you know exactly what you have to do, but it goes against everything you've told yourself you are. I'm an old man, fat from the cream and honey of a privileged life far beyond what most humans can even dare to imagine. I haven't labored with anything but my mind for decades. Surely you're the one with the advantage."

The feeling wasn't there. He needed to keep talking. "Fine, you win. Just row us back to shore. You're the bigger man here."

"Of course I'm the bigger man here. But this isn't about me. Ezra, I'm not kidding: only one of us is going back."

"If I come back with you drowned, who do you think is going to get blamed?"

"How will they know?"

"Sybil."

"She knows that if you come back I most likely will not. She's to cover for you and say you spent the entire night with her."

"Sure she is."

"Why do you think we drove your car? You row to shore, replace the boat where you found it, and drive back to the estate. She tells the authorities that I drove here on my own. Remember, she picked me up from the airport—my car's in the garage on shore. As of an hour ago you were convinced she loved you. Maybe she does. Maybe she's hoping it's you and your shitty sedan that shows up in the driveway."

"I'm supposed to believe that?"

"Are you willing to fight for her? Or is she just some fantasy you've experienced and are now bored of?"

"Fuck you."

"For all you know, she's waiting right now to see which brave knight will emerge victorious."

"She's already chosen," Ezra said. "We wouldn't be having this conversation if she hadn't."

"Thank you," Grant said. "You've officially woken up. Now, here we are. How would you like to proceed?"

He still didn't know what to do. If he attacked Grant and won, he would always envision him struggling against the current, breathing salt water into his lungs, stout body fighting for air until he succumbed. He wasn't that guy. Even if the chance to love Sybil was still possible, it wasn't something he'd kill for, or die for. There were more important things than romance.

"Do you know what she told me?" Hudson asked.

Ezra said nothing. *Keep him talking,* he thought.

"That you fucked like a boy."

"Sounds like she really wanted to convince you that I didn't matter."

"Said you had difficulty, at first, you know, making it happen."

"And you bought that line too."

"Said you needed training wheels."

Ezra didn't care about the sex. But for some reason he remembered that moment in the kitchen, when he'd come downstairs and surprised her, and she seemed really annoyed, at least at first. There couldn't have been more to that, could there? He hadn't seen her like that before. And then when they walked around the yard holding hands while his panic subsided, she got frustrated and fled. What did she really think of him?

"She said you really liked to talk about your hopes and dreams."

The theater returned, the movie. The humiliation of seeing this joke played out on-screen. All of a sudden it was clear: . she'd used him for her own pleasure and then used it to gain Grant Hudson's devotion again. He was simply a pawn in a power game between them. He'd only serve to enhance whatever sick devotion their relationship demanded.

"But funny you mentioned parents," Grant said. "Sybil said it was clear that what you really wanted was your mother."

God, he was such a fool. He began to feel the anger returning, the rage.

"Is that why you're special, Ezra? Did your momma hurt you when you were a poor little boy?"

Ezra took in all the humiliation and felt hot rage swell to his stomach, his shoulders, his throat, his eyes. He tried to stop, but couldn't. He was crying.

"You'd been doing so well," said Hudson, a little disgust now in his tone. "I thought this might be different."

Ezra wiped his nose and hocked spit over the side. He felt a limitless strength. He could knock Hudson out with one punch, row back to shore, and disappear. Or be caught and put in jail for life. Or electrocuted. He didn't care. Tears of rage blurred his eyes.

"That's enough," Grant said. "You're disgusting me."

Ezra gulped for air.

"Don't be a little bitch."

Sybil in the window, naked, with Hudson. His mother dying.

"Hey!" Hudson yelled.

Ezra looked up.

Hudson had pulled out the pistol and was holding the gun aloft, pointed just past Ezra's head. "We're done here." Hudson's lips were pursed thin. "No more games. Get the fuck over the side."

Ezra was muscle. He wanted to taste blood. He lunged and grabbed Grant's wrists, just as the pistol fired off to his right. He bore his head into Grant's chest and bit as hard as he could. He could feel, beneath the fabric of the T-shirt, flesh giving way to his teeth, and then the salty warmth of blood. Grant screamed and pushed Ezra up to standing. The boat wavered. For a moment Ezra stood, in shock, of what he'd done. He stared at Grant and saw a desperate old man on the verge of being put out of his misery.

Grant hopped up and punched him flush on the nose—pain, shock, awe—and then countered with the pistol butt to the side of the head.

Ezra toppled.

SEVENTEEN

She'd been flying again in her dreams. This time there was no sun; the cloud layer brought out the grays in every color and every shadow. She could feel the mist speckling against her face as she flew over the steep canyons pouring into the foaming surf.

And then she woke.

"Get out of bed," Grant's voice, angry. Sybil thought it was still a stress dream, her mind boiling off the anxiety of the past week. But when she opened her eyes, the room was bright. She blinked and checked the clock—it was three in the morning. He whisked the sheets off her naked body. She covered herself instinctively. "You scared me."

"Out," he said.

She didn't move. This had to be a joke. He'd done this before, pretending he was furious about something, refusing to elaborate on what. After a while, she'd realized that this was simply a tactic to make her panic and get her to confess to whatever came to mind. Overspending on clothes, unpaid traffic fines—there was never anything much. He'd relax and she'd feel ashamed, and angry, and relieved. But this? They'd just talked over everything that very afternoon. "Quit messing around."

"I'm dead serious."

Bluff. He was still trying to see how she would respond, trying to find out if she felt she deserved it. "I'm tired. Can't we play this game in the morning?" She reached over the side of the bed and pulled up the sheets he'd thrown.

He walked over to the display case and palmed one of his awards, a metal cup, and threw it against the wall. It thunked before falling softly to the carpet. She almost laughed at how anticlimactic it sounded, but didn't, because a suspicion was creeping over her that he was serious. The crevasses forming his forehead were tense but his eyes were far from fury. He touched his chest, where beneath his white shirt she could just make out a broad, rectangular bandage.

"What happened?" Even through his shirt she could see a dark stain.

He reached down and grabbed at her ankle. "Out."

She kicked his hands away. What the hell had happened to his chest? And what the fuck was he doing? On the way home from the airport they'd made resolutions to take turns supporting each other in their careers, even to make time to vacation together. They'd discussed how critical it was that they become closer than they'd ever been before, in anticipation that he might transition into politics. And they'd made love and fallen asleep together. Or at least she thought they'd fallen asleep together. "What the hell's going on?"

Grant walked into the dressing room and came out with a pile of clothes. "Get dressed. I'll send the bags wherever you end up."

"You're injured."

He didn't respond.

"Quit this. What happened? What do you think you found out?" Had he gotten in a fight with Ezra? She tried to imagine that but couldn't. But he wouldn't look at her. She pulled the pile of clothes closer and buttressed her chest and stomach with them. "I'm serious. What's wrong?"

"You're smart. You know me. Or at least you should," he said. "We've been married for over a decade."

"I don't understand."

"Clearly." He pulled out a leather chair plugged with brass buttons, flipped it around, and sat with his arms laid across the top of the backrest. "I think there's an inevitability to every-thing that happens in the world, and this has been coming for a long time now."

She hated it when he talked like this. "There's nothing with Ezra. He's gone. He never was anything. You know this."

Grant said nothing.

"What, you've been talking to him?" She'd told Grant the truth, but she'd just assumed that Ezra would do the same thing. "What did he tell you?"

"Nothing I wouldn't have guessed. But he made me realize something important." He scratched something on his hand, inspected it, and continued. "*Realize* is the wrong word. He con-firmed it in my mind, something I'd known for years. That the time had come. It arrived once you presented me with your film."

She shoved the clothes back across the bed at him. "Don't you dare go back on your promise."

"If your insistence to act and direct wasn't so desperate, it might have been passable. But even the critics would see through it. I'm comfortable making money from that film, but I'm not comfortable with my spouse representing its cause."

She backed against the headboard of the bed. "You're scared. Scared that it might come back to bite you, in some stupid, political way."

He closed his eyes and shook his head.

Sybil rose up on her knees. "You said yourself that nobody cares what kind of film I do, so long as it isn't porn."

"I lied. I'd rather you do porn than this film."

She threw a pillow at him. It glanced off his shoulder. "You're a coward."

"Am I? The film only represents my point. The problem is this: you've pitied yourself your whole life, for the precise reason no one pities you. You are a beautiful, talented, and now a wealthy woman, and you refuse to accept that people resent you for it. But not only that, deep down you realize that your *situation* on its own is not enough to garner what you really desire: sympathy. So you chose to capitalize on the tragic story of another woman in order to get what you want."

A chill pulsed through her. "How dare you? It's not as if you fought in any wars. Yet you had no problem making that sentimental trilogy the military helped fund—"

"—Don't pretend this is impersonal for you," he interrupted. "Like it is for me. Of course we as artists take the tragedies of others and with our talent and resources reshape them and profit from them. Sure, maybe we raise awareness and throw a percent or two of the profits in the direction of those afflicted. But the vast majority of the windfall is ours. We all pretend this isn't the case. Maybe pretending isn't the right word. More, *denial*. The inability—or is it unwillingness?—to face the truth. But no matter. Because even if you admitted it, deep down, the profit, the fame, and the fortune isn't enough for you. It will never be enough. This is the plague on your generation: you value victimhood over accomplishment. All the Oscars in the world couldn't stop you from examining your past, finding it privileged, and deeming yourself worthless as a result. In politics, we will get no quarter from anyone. There will be no room for victims. You would have to be above all of that. But you've shown this week what I've known all along: you can't be trusted not to sabotage our plans. I can't have any tantrums like what happened this week."

"Fuck you." She was trying to fight his words in her mind. She thought of Helen's mother, the sound of her voice all those years back when Sybil had first approached her with the idea for the film. They'd both cried together, and her tears had nothing to do with profits, with careers, with fame, or anything remotely connected with business. She'd have to call her and tell her that it was off. She'd have to tell her that it would never happen. And she'd have to explain the reasons why, and these reasons were not reasons, they were abhorrent to a mother whose daughter had gone through such a tragedy.

Then she felt a heartbreak that had nothing to do with Helen's mother, or Helen, or the injustice of it all. It didn't even have to do with the fact that she'd lost Ezra in the process, and that their brief Eden had failed because she'd sacrificed it for the promise of a different dream. No, her sorrow had to do with what would become of her career. This film, which was supposed to be her resurrection, would be her downfall.

She'd never felt this way before. There had always been something there, on the horizon, if only a glimmer of light.

There was no air in the room. Grant was a stranger. She was alone. The curtains had swung closed for good.

Grant looked at her without pity. "Get dressed. It's time to go."

Her mind felt numb. Her hands shook as she pulled on a T-shirt.

"I am leaving you with a gift."

She stopped, and for a moment, hoped. The film, regardless of what he thought of it. If she had that, this might all still be worth it.

"I have written an exposé of your life that will appear in the magazine that offers the highest bid. In it I will tell them everything. I will release the surveillance footage of you and Ezra as part of the deal. You will be shown in a terrible light. People will understand my sorrow over what happened and see my desire to leave as not only justified, but noble."

A gift? For a moment, she wondered if she was still asleep, dreaming.

"I am doing this," he continued, "because you would never do it yourself, yet it might achieve what you want. In the article, I will tell them all your faults and secrets and, at first, everyone will hate you for it. The public enjoys nothing more than burying a pathetic star. But years from now, once you have suffered sufficiently, perhaps you will finally get what you long for. Their sympathy."

The room was spinning. She closed her eyes and felt the shame carve her heart.

"Return to your family. Which is most certainly where you belong."

She felt the bed depress. He was sitting next to her.

"I will leave you to get your things—"

There was one thing he hadn't mentioned. One way in which she could feel at least some sort of relief. "What about the film?"

He stood. "Oh, right. We changed some of the backstory so that the doctor comes from Canada. I've spoken to Helen's family and they are fine with the changes. We begin filming in Vancouver six months from now. Coral Massey will play the lead."

She could barely breathe. "What right do you have to do this?"

He turned and grinned. "Right? You mean the right to do the film without you? The right to drag your name through muck? Do you really wish to discuss something so basic as rights? Sybil, who gave you the right to be beautiful? Who gave you the right to eat while others starve? To live while others die?"

He walked to the door.

"You're a monster," she said.

He paused and spoke over his shoulder. "Sure. If it helps you sleep at night."

The dizziness continued. She would be nothing. And everyone would believe that she was getting what she deserved. They would applaud.

EIGHTEEN

Ezra swam toward shore with his head above water and tried not to think, which was difficult, because it was still a long way to shore, and there was so much to try not to think about beyond the obvious danger that populated his mind through the first half hour of swimming: sharks. Now his thoughts were drawn toward death, what it felt like, and drowning, or more specifically, the moment just *before* drowning, when your body gives up while your mind is still fighting. When you're desperate to reach for the surface but your legs and arms don't respond. When you try to breathe but your lungs fill with water.

That moment when your eyes grow wide and you go still.

He needed to stop thinking.

But it was dark and the sound of the ocean slapping against him as he swam was the ticking of a clock. The top layer of water was a manageable cool, but he feared that the cool was enough to do the job. His fear felt how his mother used to describe God: with him, before him, behind him, in him. He switched between sidestroke and breaststroke to keep his eyes focused on the lights dotting the shoreline and the dull haze of the city to the south—his guides, so long as no mist or fog bank moved in, so long as the ocean currents didn't conspire to double the length of his trip or make it altogether impossible.

He had to stop thinking.

Occasionally, even with his arms growing tight, he would find a mindless rhythm. One stroke, then another, and another. But more, he fought calculations—how far, how long, at what pace—as if running through probabilities could provide a solution apart from just swimming. Meanwhile, his aching body provided its own arguments to stop.

He just needed to swim. Keep his eyes on the lights onshore, and swim.

A dull ache began to creep, first into his shoulders, next his legs. Then his left calf seized up. He sank beneath the water in pain. He felt the wash of colder water below. He struggled back to the surface and took a deep breath and went down again. While underwater, he grabbed ahold of his foot and stretched out the cramp. He rose and caught his breath, then did the same again, and again, until slowly his calf stretched out.

Out of breath, he continued on, favoring his arms, his lips parched and tasting of salt, his tongue pickled.

The shore was so far away. A shiver ran through his body. He could hear nothing but the sound of lapping water. The ocean, so casual, mocking everything he felt.

He willed himself not to think. He could make it before hypothermia set in—he had to believe that. Even if it wasn't true, what good would it do to believe otherwise?

He swam.

Soon his other calf threatened to cramp, and he found himself treading water, panting, muscles ready to coil, as much from the cold as exertion. He imagined chalky acid built up in his limbs. He closed his eyes and took a deep breath. He began floating on his back. Tried to relax. Was this it? The beginning of the end?

He forced a slow deep breath and opened his eyes. The stars glowed above him in a heavenly puzzle, and what felt like supernatural awareness warmed his senses. He blinked, doubting the sensation, but it stuck—he'd never felt more awake. He went back to treading water and looked about, anticipating a sign. Perhaps a hummingbird, or a whale, breaching up from the deep, its enormous eye making contact with his.

He waited.

But there was only darkness and waves. He sucked in breath and for a moment sank beneath the surface, into the quiet. Maybe this *was* it, and he just couldn't recognize it, because no one who had truly experienced it had ever come back to tell the tale—at least no one he could bring himself to trust.

No. He kicked to the surface again and breathed. The sea was back to its calm indifference, the shore again unreachable. Fuck. This was bullshit. He could have killed Hudson. He could be driving down the highway toward home at this very moment, needing AC instead of the coast guard. There on the boat, he'd had the advantage. But he'd hesitated. It was fucking laughable. A noble pause, and for what? No person—shit, no God in their right mind would have called that murder.

The result? Hudson could now continue with whatever psycho plans he surely had brewing, while Ezra, friend to all, swam for his life.

Fucking hilarious.

As he treaded water, the pleasure of irony faded to the reality of his doom. He needed help. A plank of stray wood, a mass of kelp bulbs, anything to hold on to. Weren't there countless islands of trash scattered across the ocean, each of them miles long? How was there nothing here, spitting distance from the largest city on the West Coast?

Again, from nowhere, that strange awareness struck him dizzy, that sense of connection to the world, of being a part of Planet Fucking Earth and the Milky Way and the universe and some mind that thought it all up. Yes, it was true, it was all true, and it suddenly felt so obvious. God existed and was making shit happen and you just had to open your eyes to see it. Finally his eyes were open too. Why hadn't it felt this way for him until now?

It occurred to him that it probably had to do with the fact that he was about to die. But he prayed and felt a calm assurance. In his mind, a dolphin appeared, and he felt hope. Perhaps his mother had sent it, from beyond the grave, from heaven. He'd once heard a tale that dolphins were able to save people. Maybe it wasn't a tale. Anything seemed possible. He willed that he might suddenly hear water gushing from a blow-hole, and that he might simply grab a dorsal fin and be carried through the waves to shore.

He waited. Like he had on the shore of the Atlantic, all those years ago, both hoping and fearing that the Apocalypse might finally come, he waited. But again the feeling of reverence diminished to nothing, and here he was, in the water, nobody special, shivering.

Then he remembered something he'd learned in a survival camp he'd attended as a kid. He could use his jeans as a flotation device. He struggled to strip them from his body, tied up both pant legs, and flipped their heavy dampness over his head like one might flick a sheet over a mattress. To his surprise, they filled with a decent pocket of air.

He cried and laughed. What the hell. A few more minutes of life. He lay on his back with the jeans gripped to his chest and floated. His ears sank beneath the water while his eyes, nose, and mouth stayed above. He looked up into the stars and wondered how it might sound in heaven, if heaven was indeed more than a wish. Would it be like the dead quiet of outer space? Or would the air be how his mother insisted: thick with the sound of voices and the smell of nature redeemed from all the sin that humanity had brought about. Humans and birds finally reconciled. People and earth finally one.

The moment in his past he fought hardest to forget but always remembered visited him once again. That door he could never shut. That light he could never turn off. That sound he could never mute. He was fourteen, horizontal, facing the sky just as he was now in the ocean, only on the solid ground of the mountain forest. Matted needles from the towering red pines overhead dug into his back. His hands crusaded around the naked chest of the teenage lifeguard who was in the process of changing his life. His pants were already stained, but he was still as hard as the pitiless young saplings springing up from the old stumps all around him. She ground her hips into him and shoved her bubble gum tongue deep inside his mouth. He welcomed her search. Boy, did he. A respite from the spiral his mother seemed to be in. A respite from the church camp he still was forced to attend, even though everyone hated him.

Earlier that day, in the pool, all the boys had been circled around some kid with his eyes closed pretending to be blind. The kid called out Marco and took leaps of faith toward the chorus of voices yelling Polo, all skylarking about, dodging contact, a pack of little trickster gods mocking a blind, earnest believer. Ezra hovered on the outside of the circle, watching. But he wasn't interested, not anymore, and not just because these people were no longer his friends. Up on the white picket lifeguard tower sat a girl whose amber legs flickered in the may-fly-thick afternoon sun.

Ezra floated toward the tower and pulled himself onto the side of the pool. Soon there was a switching of the guard, and she was seated next to him, those legs dangling in the cool sapphire. Soon they were on their way to discovering that both of their parents were religious leaders, and that they were tired of the pressure to live up to expectations. They discovered that what both of them wanted was precisely the kind of companionship their elders had warned against. Something to make them feel like more than just a soul. Something that would make them feel human.

She was awkward. She scratched his shoulder with her fake nails, and when rolling over, elbowed him in the ribs. He accidently pulled her hair while trying to massage her scalp, and squeezed her chest too hard, making her wince. This was not pretty. This was not clean. This was not romantic. But it felt miraculous.

He'd been told his whole life that the greater world held only suffering and damnation . . . but God, what a world. He snorted for breath and smelled pine sap as she once again buried her face into his like a shovel into sand, while down in camp, outside of view, the kids played dodgeball, made quilts, and held hands to pray.

She had just taken a tiny nip of his chin when something startled him. The black honey smell of burning wood. He glanced past her thick curls and spotted, to the side, dissipating into the clear hot mountain air, funnels of gray smoke.

Sirens screamed. They both unwrapped themselves and stumbled to their feet and saw smoke rushing up to the heavens. They dressed. She leaped onto the trail and ran. He followed her to the edge of the hill and saw orange light peeking out below from between midsummer pines. The smoke darkened to slate and the wind shifted, obscuring the sun.

They hurtled down the trail toward camp, nettles and bushes tearing at their legs. The sirens grew louder with each step. They split off at the huge wooden water tower, her down a trail toward the pool, and Ezra toward the fire. He wove between cabins and passed clusters of kids, keeping his eye on the smoky plume. Soon he was in its perimeter and he coughed at its invisible thickness, from which kids and counselors were scattering in all directions.

Then the fire. How fascinating the fire. He felt less fear than wonder.

He pushed his way to the front of a small crowd, full of wringing hands ill-equipped for heroics. Cabin Omega flared a beautiful, picturesque orange. And out of it hurdled a person impossibly ablaze, somehow still on two feet, hurtling toward the crowd.

Toward him.

And there the memory stopped. And always his mind went next to the picture she'd shown him of the burning monk the month before. And from there to all of the moments she'd spoken of how no one had ears to hear and eyes to see. That the world needed a symbol. And how he'd done nothing.

She'd left no letter. She'd said goodbye to him in the same manner that she'd said goodbye to everyone else there at the camp. She'd finally become her message, as she'd always wanted to. Even to him, the one person who knew her best. She'd made him the son of a symbol.

There in the quiet ocean, he began to sob, at first in fits, then uncontrollably. What would it feel like to want to disappear like that? Not simply to end your life, but to erase yourself out of your own story? It was unimaginable. He could never understand it. God, it hurt to not understand. It only proved how far from her he'd become by the end. If he could just could go back and somehow save her from that unspeakable pain and whatever had caused it, or even just to understand it. He would give anything.

If only there was someone to give it to. Someone to pay.

He'd lost her, that pain only a rehearsal for what he'd struggled with every day since: missing her. Yes, out here at the end of it, he knew: it wasn't losing her, it was missing her that had changed his life. Missing her that had brought him here. Missing her that had made him into the person he was, and wasn't. Those moments he called back, the gymnasium, that night he discovered the nature of his father, that day at summer camp when he'd lost her . . . he'd been treating them as clues to who he was, clues to his destiny, his character, his identity. But those were only distractions from the larger struggle, weren't they? The most important clue was this: he couldn't stop playing those scenes over and over in his head. He couldn't get rid of them, couldn't let them go—that was their power. They weren't about who he was. They were about who he missed, and how deeply he ached for her presence.

When she died, he broke. The leadership of the church deemed it a martyrdom, and the church was invigorated, and once more he was treated with reverence. The elders approached him, recognizing him as a Prophet too.

You have her gift. You share her pain. We can see it.

They believed it. They really did. They were all so earnest in their apologies, their confessions, and their humility. He could have hated them for it, maybe even loved them. As it was, he didn't feel anything at all. He wasn't ready to face it, nor did he know how.

So, he'd left. For three years, he roamed west, farther and farther away. He found manual labor on farms throughout the Midwest. Stayed for a season and hitchhiked, then another, and another, until finally he'd found the fertile grounds of the Central Valley. He worked the field and once again moved on, to a vineyard on the coast, and after that, to the city, and this.

But why had he stayed? Of all the places in the world, here, instead of alone in the rainforests of the South Pacific with his camera, where his heart yearned to go?

His sobbing slowed. He knew. He knew. There was something about his mother, Grant, and Sybil that he hadn't understood until now. This need to shine brighter than other people. This need to fill more space than others. To be important. Powerful. To rise above convention. To transcend any definition of normal. To be more than just a human being.

It was an escape.

Why had his mother allowed people to call her the Prophetess? Why hadn't she just let them call her by her real name?

Why had she felt the need to inhabit her message, to become a symbol, rather than to stay in this world with him?

An escape.

Sybil. Grant. This whole town. This whole world. What was being accomplished?

Escape.

There was no one left to fool, here in the ocean, alone and on the verge of dying. His being here, wasn't it for the same reasons as them? He was no different. Trying for some sort of secret glory, not through accomplishment, but through severe self-discipline. Had he not stood upon his own private pedestal and looked down at Bryce and April and the rest of them and felt pride that *at least he wasn't them*?

An escape, not from the world, but from the fact that he missed her, and couldn't bear to face it.

He sobbed.

He was the same. They were all the same. Everyone.

But that no longer mattered. He closed his eyes. Any insights now were meaningless. He would soon be gone, and there'd be no place to spend their gold. He'd leave, and if he was lucky, join her in a place where any knowledge of this world was beside the point. His muscles were so tired and he felt a warmth in his body that could be nothing less than a stage of hypothermia. The salt of the air, a breath of wind on his face—they conjured a feeling similar to making out with that girl in summer camp all those years ago.

He opened his eyes and saw a satellite blinking across the horizon. Impressive, but not when compared to the millions of bright and dim stars and who knew what else behind it, all those unthinkable miles away, nor his cold, miraculous skin sending message after message to his brain. And his heart, still beating without permission.

He smiled. Shivered. Death was here. What else could he do but smile? He closed his eyes.

NINETEEN

Late that morning, Sybil slid the plastic key through the scanner and strolled through the hotel suite. She felt such clarity. Cocaine and wine and not giving a fuck did that to a person. She finally, at long last, understood the world. And once a person understands the world, they'll understand who they'll never be.

She flipped on the overhead lights and dropped the satchel on the bed, then lay down and stared at the ceiling. The garish wallpaper was a strain of yellow similar to the backdrop behind Helen in the video. Who could have predicted that Helen would have been this particular kind of inspiration? And Ezra's mother? As Ezra'd said, it was uncanny, but more so than he could have ever known.

She struggled up from the bed and stumbled to the bathroom, satchel in hand. There was nothing left to lose. Marriage? Check. Career? Check. Lover? Check.

Beauty? She looked in the mirror; her face was pale and her eyes had a pinkish sheen. It was not difficult to imagine the skeleton beneath. Beauty, what her fame was built on, the only reason people had ever cared, was on its way out. She punched the mirror, which barely budged, and rubbed her knuckles.

The fake lemon smell of industrial cleaner hit her nose. She closed her eyes and for a moment felt as though she was swimming in the ocean, swells passing her by. She shook it off and unzipped the suitcase, removing an extra-large box of D batteries and a hacksaw. She set them both on the rim of the bathtub.

Before checking into the hotel, she'd driven through the city and seen it as she'd never seen it before. Dry. Cracked. Thirsty. Pleas for help scrawled on van windows. *Wash me.*

She'd found a hardware store with a faded sign. The clerk clearly knew who she was; she could see it in his smirk, his silence. She didn't belong there, any more than she belonged in that mansion.

Hah! She didn't belong anywhere, except on billboards, centerfolds, and screens. No one wanted her around, except when they were alone, having sex with themselves. She was the opposite of platonic, and when she tried to be otherwise, was met with disdain, if not anger.

Hudson and Ezra never loved her. They were only living out in real life the fantasies of millions of other men and women both distracted and comforted by an ideal. In that way, she realized, she *was* platonic—a puppet whose ideal form was cast in shadow on a wall, to be yearned for and enjoyed without any semblance of relationship.

Hacksaw. Batteries. Their weight so thrilling in her hands. This is what defiance felt like.

She tore at the plastic edges of the battery pack, but it was sealed together with a sharp stamped edge. She held the pack sideways on the sink and with the saw scraped her way through, until there was a large enough gap that she could peel the plastic apart. A few of the batteries spilled out and pooled in the sink while the rest stayed snug in the package. She fingered the first fat cylinder and laid it sideways on the granite countertop of the sink.

But she'd forgotten her phone. She walked into the bedroom and plucked it from the nightstand. The plan was to stream this live. She would pin back her hair and with her rouge brush apply the acidic powder to her cheeks. Then wait. Viewers wouldn't know what was happening. They would watch it work in real time, eating its way through her cheeks, her chin, her nose, her forehead. Not her eyes, though. They'd be a perfectly clear, unblemished reminder of what had surrounded them before.

In a way, she was just intending to speed up the violence that time had planned to do all along. She'd be a living reminder of that fact. Instead of trying to look young, like everyone else, she'd do the opposite. Instead of slowly fading, she would brand herself into the American consciousness. The real world wouldn't let her show on film what she felt in real life, so she'd perform it, live, for everyone. They'd see and never forget the reality that Helen felt, and she felt, and would soon feel in full.

She took her phone and propped it against a stack of rectangle bars of soap, camera facing her. She removed her clothes. Dimmed the lights. Gripped the hacksaw and pressed its sharp, tiny teeth into one of the smooth batteries. They sunk into the soft plastic. She pushed and felt the blade saw against the metallic insides. Then she lost the grip and the blade jumped and the battery rattled into the basin of the sink.

Her hands were shaking. She looked up into the mirror and saw a single drop of blood slowly descend from her nostril, followed by a trail of more. The drip crested over the edge of her lips and down into her mouth. She licked it and tasted the salt. She tried to pick up the saw again, press the blade down, but the thick shell of the battery again slipped on the porcelain.

"Fuck me." She sat down on the edge of the bathtub and put her head between her knees. An image came into her mind—that of the monk burning himself—brought on by the story Ezra had told about her mother's self-immolation. What had Ezra said about her? *She wanted the world to know her pain. She wanted the world to know her.* But instead of expressing that to one person at a time, and growing closer, she'd pushed them away and chosen the opposite: infamy.

It occurred to Sybil that she was choosing something similar. She felt guilty. Ashamed. She tried to banish the feelings, but that only made her feel disoriented, like a stranger to herself. When she wiped her nose and mouth with the back of her hand, it smeared with blood and snot.

The camera, tilted up against the soap, ready to record, now scared her. What would people say? A desperate cry for attention. A grab at fame when she felt it slipping away. An abomination to use the suffering of Helen, who'd been scarred against her will, as inspiration.

There was, she realized, some truth to that.

Truth that Grant would dismiss. He'd say this was simply turning suffering into a commodity. No big deal. This was simply what artists did, and should do, as a service to humankind, because those truly suffering inevitably had neither the time, resources, nor talent to fashion their experiences into art. She realized that in a way, he was also right.

Art was never pure. Hadn't ever been. Even cave drawings from thousands of years before made audiences swoon, and as a result, relationships and goods were won.

The bathroom spun, but her thoughts felt more than clear.

Yes, she'd told herself this was purely a statement, even performance art, but what about those delusions of grandeur she'd imagined: the news, the documentaries . . . the question *why did she do it* on everyone's lips. A sudden burst of fame. A resurrection through suffering. This was a power grab as much as a statement. Self-preservation as much as self-immolation.

But trading fame for infamy would have the same result. Her new pedestal would become even more of a cage than her beauty. A year from now, the same question would remain. Even ten years from now. *Why did she do it?* There'd be no other part left to play, only this symbol.

As she sat there on the edge of the bathtub, in the suite in one of the nicest hotels in Tinseltown, she imagined the years ahead of her. If she decided not to go through with it—which, to be honest, was all but decided—she'd have to embrace the slow fade, less beauty, less fame. Less attention from the paparazzi, from the Internet, from everyone.

But who knew? Perhaps in place of her career, she'd find what she had with Ezra: love. Real connection. What she wanted. A belonging not based on looks or achievement. What Helen had, before it all became too much—having so much taken in an instant, instead of over time, or by choice. Yes, she owed Helen and her family, but not for the reasons she'd first assumed.

It was time to come to terms with the fact that the life she'd hoped for was no longer possible. She needed to accept that and move on. Trust that other possibilities would arise, and that what she lost would be replaced by something different, perhaps not better, but maybe, just maybe, good.

She took a few Kleenex, wiped her face, and gazed into the mirror.

She gathered the batteries and threw them, one by one, into the garbage. She chuckled. It occurred to her that she didn't even know whether they could have done the job.

TWENTY

Ezra heard gentle beeps and the whoosh of recycled air. The light was dim through the cracks in the drapes. He blinked and saw a tall vase of bright carnations. Beside them, Maria, wearing dark-purple scrubs. He wondered whether she was a ghost, whether he was too. His headache didn't feel as though it was from the afterlife, and neither did the look of her eyes: a little dark and bothered, but caring. His head was still swimming; probably if he tried to stand he would fall. "What happened?"

"Welcome back." She stood and flipped on the lights, which at first felt blinding.

He didn't know quite what to think. He searched his memory. The boat? The swim? Had he dreamed those? Or had he passed out somewhere downtown after—oh God—the movie theater. He closed his eyes. Those memories felt like a dream, but so did Maria. He now wished she were just an anonymous staff person. "Are you my doctor?"

"Physician's assistant. And nope, I work a few floors up. Shift ended a couple hours ago. One of the nurses tipped me off you were here. You've been in the news."

"Hah," he said, but by the look on her face, she might not be kidding. He didn't want to know, at least not yet. He felt so tired. And thirsty. He glanced over and saw that the teal hospital breakfast tray on the side table was empty, except for a few crumbs on the plastic plate and an unused straw next to the plastic cup.

"Hope you don't mind that I ate," she said. "I was hungry and you were out. I can get you more."

"Maybe some water?" He reached for it and realized there were loose harnesses holding down his arms and legs, along with IVs stuck into the pit of his elbow.

"You're strapped in," she said. "Until you can prove to the psychologist that going for a swim alone in the middle of nowhere in the middle of the night wasn't, well."

They were worried he'd tried to commit suicide. "Where did I come to shore?"

"Luma." She picked up the water and fit the straw to his mouth.

He felt marginally embarrassed being fed, but drank, nearly draining the tinted plastic cup. He then closed his eyes. He'd drifted all the way south to Luma. Public, insanely popular, easy to access—no one would assume he hadn't swum out from there as well—nothing to tie him to Grant's place. "The last couple of days seem like someone else's life."

"Try again. You've been laying here for almost four days." Her look told him she wasn't kidding. "The records say a life-guard was out running with his dog at four in the morning and found you lying just below the tide line. Negligible heartbeat. Low temperature. Dehydrated. Another hour and you would have died."

So his memories were all true. Everything. He remembered nothing after deciding to float. How did he get to shore? How did he hold on to his jeans? Had he, in some state of oblivion, turned over and begun swimming again? Had the current swept him onto shore? "So how did I survive . . . ?"

She shrugged. "You tell me. I don't even know what the heck you were doing."

There was a gap. He hadn't had one before. As crazy as it sounded, it unnerved him more than being locked down in the hospital, on IVs. He'd existed without being conscious of existing, not just during the time in the water but the last three days. Every move, every word, every thought had been so tightly governed, and now, a gap—at precisely the moment when it could have proved what he most wanted to know.

She smiled. "Don't worry about all of that now. Just worry about getting better. How are you feeling? Are you in pain?" And with her voice the image of April, at Bryce's apartment, wearing only Bryce's T-shirt, popped into his mind. He glanced down at Maria's hands. There was no ring.

She held up her empty fingers for him. "I understand you already know."

He searched her face for pain, but found none. And she was working, covering a shift, at most four days after finding out. "I'm sorry. I would have—"

"—Really, it's fine." She crossed her arms.

It occurred to him how many times throughout his life he'd said *it's fine* when the truth was the opposite. He suspected she didn't mean it, either.

"No," she said. "It is. Really. We had our doubts. Even him asking me . . . it was a surprise. I know how it looked at the restaurant. 'Yay, true love!'" She took a deep breath and turned her back to him. "I wanted it to be that way. But it wasn't real. A part of me just wanted it to be. That's something I'm guilty of a lot."

"You're not alone in that." Ezra shook his head. "Anyway, I'm sorry. I had no idea."

She stood up, eyes wide. "Really? I figured you knew all this. I figured that's why you left us at the diner."

"Honestly, I didn't know."

She studied him. He could feel it in her gaze, the question: *then why did you leave?*

"Bryce could see the end and was afraid. He's a fearful guy and hides it well. And April, well, you've seen how they are together."

Ezra nodded, more as a reflex than anything else. He'd seen none of it, and even when he scoured his memory, trying to piece it together from evidence, no. He'd missed it completely. "Both of you seemed genuine."

"We can be good at seeming." She walked over to the sink and refilled his water. She wiped something off the counter, crossed her arms, and shrugged. "Well, then this will be news as well. No offense, but April going after you wasn't just pure, unbridled attraction. Let's just say you're not her first, and she got what she was after in the end."

He blinked. The whole time he'd been worried about taking advantage of April when she had been taking advantage of him. He'd been so concerned with his own actions he'd completely misjudged hers. And Bryce's. Shit, everyone's. He'd assumed simplicity in everyone but himself. All that self-loathing had disguised his own arrogance.

She smiled and shook her head, eyes now reaching for the corner of the room. "I just stuck around for some reason. But look at me. You're strapped to a gurney and I'm the one unloading on you."

It occurred to him that this world might not be as lonely as he'd thought. He smiled, but doing so triggered something in his jaw that made his head hurt more. Coughing overtook him and he began to retch. He tried to bring his hand to his mouth but couldn't, and he felt phlegm running down his lips. She nabbed a few paper towels from the dispenser and wiped his mouth.

"I'm disgusting," he said.

"I've seen much worse." She dabbed at his mouth and his chin.

The way her eyes studied him, trying to find anything else that needed to be cleaned up, brought up emotions he wasn't expecting. "Thank you," he said as she wiped the spit from his robe and threw away the towels.

She sat back down and wheeled the chair next to the bed. She reached out and took his hand, which was warm and soft. He found himself trying to find an ulterior motive to her holding his hand. He wondered what that was about—this desire to dismiss a caring gesture from a friend as manipulative. He'd missed so much lately, so much that was apparently obvious to people he trusted and respected, like Maria.

"So tell me what happened. If you're feeling up to it, of course."

He tried, but the fatigue clouded his mind. He found he could talk somewhat clearly about Sybil and Grant, but when it came to himself and his past, he struggled to find words. "Of

course, there's more. There's just so much I've never told you.
Never really told anyone."

She nodded. "I'm realizing that. And you're not alone, by
the way. I have a past."

He squeezed her hand. "I feel like I should apologize."

"Don't." She squeezed his hand back and pulled away, smiling slightly, without showing teeth. Her skin was smooth and
her eyebrows were just the tiniest bit bushy. Hair in a ponytail. They were silent and he began to feel that he'd shared too
much. That she'd leave the room, her eyes would grow big, and
she'd hope she'd never see him again.

"What about Sybil?" he asked. The moment he asked, he
felt the desire to preface the comment by saying how he felt
about Sybil's betrayal, how they were over, how he didn't want
her back.

There was a knock at the door and a nurse entered the room.
She nodded at Maria and smiled at Ezra. "You're awake!"

Maria was staring at him as if she was deciding whether to
tell him something important. But she got up to leave.

"Wait," he said.

"You've got a lot of resting up to do," Maria said. "I'll
make sure they take good care of you." She turned to go, but
stopped, not quite facing him, but not quite facing away, either.
"I'm back on at midnight. I can come back a little early to visit."

Yes, he thought. *Please do.* Was it possible to miss someone's presence while they were still in the room? *Please do.* But
at the same time there were dozens of phrases on his tongue,
ones he'd picked up from who knew how many stories because
they'd mimed the fear he'd felt so many times before. His entire
life, really. Phrases that would create distance, ones he'd used so

often that he didn't even think about them: *I'll be okay. No, I'll be fine. You're too kind, but it's really all right. Thanks, that's okay. No worries. I'll let you know.*

"Thanks," he said. "It would mean a lot."

She smiled and left as the nurse began her examination.

TWENTY-ONE

Two afternoons before, in the patio outside the mansion, Grant Hudson was basting a mix of molasses, mango, and peppers onto a curved rack of ribs. The sun filtered through the palms and yellow jackets were already pestering the meat and the sauce. Grant licked his fingers and felt the bite of the habanero blot out the sweetness. The party was due to begin in a few hours but the suck-ups would arrive early, as they always did. He could see their smiles now. They would inquire about the absence of his lovely wife and he would direct them to read the papers, as if they hadn't already.

The barbecue would be a show of strength, a chance for him to dismiss their condolences and whispered pity. This was a critical moment, because pity could be beneficial only if a person could show how little they needed it. Linger too long in it, people began to see you and the pity as the same thing. A lesser man might have rented out a ballroom, paid for the best bands, and dropped six figures to save face. The guests would enjoy it, but those with sway would say that he was trying too hard, and speculate as to why—and for good reason. They knew how quickly pity could turn to condescension, and how delightful that turn could be, to those who might benefit.

But an intimate gathering for a barbecue and drinks at the house? Just the right amount of personal touch. It would help everyone feel that they were part of an inner circle, rather than a statement, a staged event, or worse, a cry for help.

It took both of Grant's hands to flip the enormous rack of ribs over on the aluminum foil. He felt a slight pain in his shoulder. Soreness from clocking Ezra. The bite mark on his chest hadn't healed, either. But those were small payments. He felt sated. Ezra's payment was a private near-drowning that dovetailed perfectly with Sybil's public one, which was happening at that very moment, through every news outlet in the free world. It made a wonderful pattern, as the first act of his life years ago had closed with a kind of drowning, as well.

He entertained that memory while ladling gobs of the sauce onto the rack. It had been an unseasonably warm fall day in the breadbasket of the inland Pacific Northwest, those endless, rolling seas of agriculture, each field nearly the size of a sea. It was sunny and cold, and this far north darkness fell early. He was twenty, still went by Frederick, and was traveling in the back seat of a shiny yellow coupe that belonged to his future namesake, who was at the wheel.

His mother sat in the passenger seat, wearing tan leather boots and a matching leather jacket, beneath which a marbled silk shirt flared. Tight jeans and an absurdly large belt buckle with turquoise stones. Hair feathered. The elder Grant Hudson had ditched his Big Apple attire and was now wearing designer bell-bottom jeans, boots made from an unknown species, and a large coat lined with fur.

They'd both ditched their names, twice over, and it took a couple of years, but he'd found them. So he smuggled them, at gunpoint, from the parking lot of a hotel named after a piece of furniture. During the hour-and-a-half ride south along empty roads bordering resting soil, he'd learned little about both of their lives. Hudson had told his wife not to speak, and she hadn't, which in some regard made sense, considering the way they lived their lives. But this was Frederick's mother, there in the front seat, in the flesh, and he hadn't seen her for years. Of all things, he hadn't expected this. Back in the parking lot, when he first confronted them, she appraised him once and that was it. What mother didn't care to know—*yearn* to know, even— about the doings of her own child? Couldn't fear even stoke her maternal instinct?

It had taken a while—years—but eventually, Frederick had come to understand what she'd done, or at least believed he had. She'd come upon a chance for a new name and life, with no connections to the mistakes she'd made before. The fresh start was one of privilege and affluence far beyond what she could have ever dreamed. So she took it, without Frederick, for fear his coming might eventually change Hudson's mind.

Still, Frederick had always harbored hope that she had a larger plan. She'd someday come back, asking for him, and they'd embrace, and she'd apologize, and she'd reveal what she'd been through to make certain his future was better than hers. Believing that helped him sleep at night.

But there in the yellow coupe, as more miles of fallow fields passed in silence, that hope began to fade, and he began to feel foolish. He'd built a statue to his mother in his mind, like those in the church he was made to go to as a child, of Mary doting over young Jesus. There was little else solid in his world, but he'd always banked on this being true: mothers loved their children, to a fault. They couldn't help it. It was a mysterious, strange virtue. A truth that even his pain couldn't spoil.

In his fantasies, throughout the years of toil and disappointment, he'd often imagined her taking a step outside the window onto the deck of a posh suite at the top of some high rise in a huge metropolis. There she looked into the moon and stars dimmed by the lights of the city, and thought of her son. He imagined prayers from her lips and regret in her heart—how many times had he borne the brunt of his father's rage, so that it might be spent on him instead of her?

Any hint of feeling for anyone else had long since been beaten out of Frederick. But for her, his heart still cracked. And over time, that crack had expanded to crevasse, and the crevasse to a canyon, and the canyon to a gulf, until he could stand it no more.

So here he was. Ready to rid his mother of Grant Hudson. Expecting her joy and embrace.

But here she was, feet from him, and silent.

The only way he could bear what was unfolding in Hudson's coupe was to hound them with stories of what had been happening in town since they'd disappeared with everyone's money and trust. How a good portion of the population moved away. How a desperate few—bankrupt, foreclosed, too old to start over—had taken their lives to spare themselves and their loved ones the cost of the wait. There were those who'd found solace in vices. And then there were those like him who'd forged documents so they could sign on, far too young, to brave the nor'easters fishing and line up outside the one cannery left in town.

Once he finished telling them all that their actions had has-tened, Frederick said, from the back seat, "This is one hell of a car. I would have expected some sort of thank you."

Hudson, steering around yet another bare road straddling the empty hills, finally spoke. "How do you figure that?"

"I paid for it. We paid for it. My father and I and everyone else you screwed."

"Keep telling yourself that," Hudson said. "If it wasn't me, it'd be someone else. And from what I saw of you and your father and the rest of that town, I was only helping you along toward the inevitable."

His mother said nothing. Didn't even turn around. Freder-ick couldn't believe it.

"Turn left up here," he said, tapping the pistol against his namesake's head.

Hudson complied. "Where are we going?"

Frederick said nothing.

"I'll stop unless you answer me."

Frederick bashed the butt of the pistol into Hudson's skull. Hudson yelled and the car swerved before continuing on.

"Keep driving," Frederick said. "I'd just as soon kill you. But your life is in her hands."

Still his mother didn't move. A thought occurred to him, one he'd entertained before and dismissed as folly. Maybe she was so demoralized that she was afraid to even speak. Perhaps he, Frederick, was now in the same position that Hudson had been in all those years ago. History repeated itself. That crack in his heart stayed open.

This was the plan, one Frederick had deliberated on for months. He would kidnap them both, take them out to someplace quiet and reserved, and threaten them with their lives, until they both told the truth. He needed to know what had happened all of these years. And most importantly, why she hadn't come back for him.

He'd hoped it wouldn't come anywhere near that far—the driving, the threatening. That when his mother saw him and felt him near, she'd be grateful.

But there in the car, God, it was shameful, he realized. It took a kidnapping and a gun to get the truth? Fuck, who was he? Some sort of demon child? What had he done, except exist—and whose choice was that? Hers and his father's.

All he wanted was for someone on this planet to care.

She didn't move.

They drove, up and down the hills, into the belly of a field, gravel skittering beneath the wheels. The sun had nearly set. They were miles from anything, but he saw a small pond there in the distance.

"Take a right at that break in the road," Frederick said. "Isn't this fun? It's like we're on a road trip together. One big happy family."

"You don't know nothing about the world," Hudson said. "You haven't a clue how it works."

"Whatever you say. But we love games, don't we, Mom? It's in our name."

She said nothing.

Back in the patio, a yellow jacket landed on the meat and Hudson bashed it with the handle of the brush until only its tiny legs quaked in death throes. He pinched its head between his fingers and tossed it into the heart of the grill, where the insect sizzled and popped.

Frederick stopped the car next to the pond and ordered them to get out. They complied and stood there, cold breath clouding their faces.

"Explain yourself," he told his mother. "Now."

"Explain what?"

"You know what."

"I've made my decisions and stuck by them. You've a right to call me selfish, but I can live with that. I've lived with far more—far more than you ever saw. Your father couldn't understand that the world didn't exist to give him favors."

"I don't give a shit about my father."

"Then what the hell do you want?"

He could feel the emotions stirring inside; he hated them. "What about me? Fuck. I was young."

"Oh, please. I could see it in you from the day you came flailing out of me. You've always been your father's son. Crying. Pouting. Always trying to be like him. Then trying to take his place. Thinking you could protect me. You want the truth, here it is: I lived my life around people going nowhere, and I was tired of it. You were a boy but I already knew what kind of man you'd make. This here only proves it."

She continued talking, in a fury, shaming him for even questioning her freedom to do whatever she pleased with her life. As she kept talking he felt himself cool down to the point where he didn't feel anything about her, anything at all, unless you could call disdain a feeling—but to him, it was more like a thought.

That this woman in front of him was no longer worth his time. But by the look in Grant Hudson's eyes, he knew she'd served a purpose.

"—So fine, big Mr. Chance," his mother said. "You want a fucking game?" she said.

"Sure, whenever you're done whining," Frederick said.

"Name the fucking rules," she said.

It came to Frederick there, in an instant, an epiphany of sorts. He looked back and forth between his mother and Grant Hudson and no longer found any reason not to entertain it.

"Hudson," Frederick said. "If you kill my mother, you can go free."

There was a moment of silence. But then Hudson did, with his bare hands. Frederick didn't expect it to happen so quickly, so matter-of-fact. It was awful. But less so than he thought it would be. And to watch it happen at his request sparked something inside of him.

After it was done, Frederick shot Hudson and buried them both in the soft shore of the pond. It took him nearly eight hours to do it right, but he was fit and not a soul came anywhere near. He left, and soon the pond froze, and with it, that last crack in his heart. The bodies were never found and nothing was made of their disappearance, as they'd been disappearing their entire lives.

Frederick had decided, driving back from the pond all those years ago, to be a conductor. One of those who never did the dirty work themselves. One of those who understood that once you could find out what someone really wanted—or even better, what they really loved—you could use that sentiment to win their trust, and turn them into an ally, which was only one step away from becoming a servant. And soon they'd bow, perhaps even thank you for the opportunity, because you'd helped give them what they wanted. Each of them not thinking for a moment of the shackles they'd put around their own wrists to get it.

He wasn't a *Chance*. No mere luck would ever again determine his fate. He was the man in the white Detroit bull that everyone wanted to be like. The one that mothers would choose over their sons. Someone able to remove anything or anyone from his life with a calm demeanor. One free to pursue his desires and dreams without hesitation or hindrance. He took the name Grant Hudson. Willing to do anything to secure his fate, only far smarter in his cunning. And the name had a certain ring to it.

And today, it was time for Act Three of Grant Hudson's life to begin. Once the hullabaloo about Sybil died down, he would return east, reveal his past, change his name back to Frederick Chance, and the truth of his pitiable upbringing would only add to his legend. A poor boy, abandoned by his mother, orphaned by his father, works his way up through blue-collar America and finds success and fame among the royalty of America. But betrayed by one of the elite—his wife, no less—he returns to his roots and decides he's had enough of the glitz and the glamour and wants to work to make the world better for that poor young orphan with forged papers who works long hours at a cannery, not just so he can eat but so he can retain what Americans value more than anything else: independence.

None of the bureaucrats knew any of this. Not yet. They'd been busy trying to milk him for campaign finances. They wanted to be conductors themselves. Why let an outsider in on their nepotistic game? But he'd kept the papers and the records of his birth and travels. Spun right, his mother's disappearance might even add to the miraculous nature of his story.

He'd misled Ezra about memoirs. Only the final chapter of his was yet to be written. He'd have his choice of publishers. The powerful in the press junket already owed him favors. A year from now it would begin. He'd leap over the bureaucrats and into the arms of the people. What was wonderful about America was that people voted for the best story, if only to prove, once every couple of decades, that they weren't beholden to the family legacies that all other nations were. They loved the outsider. Grant didn't need a forecast. His governor's term would be interrupted by a run for the presidency. They'd beg him to do it. He'd decline until he'd gathered enough of their warm loyalty to win and win again.

The phone in his pocket buzzed. He ignored it. Then he wondered if maybe it was Sybil, so he checked it, but no, it was that ghoul of an accountant from the studio wanting an update on numbers. Sybil was probably gone, off to find herself; he'd seen the charges on their credit cards. Tickets home to Seattle purchased. Over the last decade, she'd become what she wanted, only to find out she didn't like what she'd become. He'd get no thanks. But he'd also get no vitriol, because it was in their prenuptial agreement that she wouldn't reveal any-thing—only he got that privilege. In time, she'd realize it hadn't been as bad as her isolation and failures had led her to think. Once she'd experienced worse, and seen him experiencing so much better, perhaps she'd come crawling back. Then, more fun.

Which reminded him: one of his tasks now was to find another mate in search of a husband in whom she could find self-worth. Bachelors had only been president twice, and each of their legacies was negligible. He needed another climber with the wit to rule others but the insecurity to need a father's love and encouragement to succeed. They were everywhere, but few were like Sybil: smart enough to doubt herself to the point of distrust, tragic enough to imagine a golden heart within everyone, and hopeful enough to trust that with enough effort, everything would work out in the end. She'd been perfect for a guy of his sensibilities. Perfect for Act Two. But she lacked nobility.

Everything went a shade darker. He looked up into the sky and noticed something he hadn't seen since he'd left New York: dark clouds. A carpet of them, moving in from the coast, blocking the sun and nearly overhead. He hoped it wouldn't rain. That might ruin the barbecue. But then again, it might make the party memorable, add significance to the occasion. The first rain in months, bringing the promise of new life.

Another couple of wasps showed up to sniff the meat. Grant swatted at them but they weren't intimidated. He basted the last few spots of the rack and lifted it onto the second level of the grill. Sauce dripped and chattered on the hot irons. He tossed in a few handfuls of applewood chips that had been soaking in a bucket for good measure. He shut the grill and licked the sauce from his fingers.

A hummingbird appeared a dozen yards away, in one of the groves of the garden. It darted from flower to flower, looking mechanical, like one of those automated machines in the airplane manufacturing plant he had a stake in just south. He thought of Ezra. What a lost soul. He'd survived. No matter. That boy didn't have the balls to seek revenge, nor enough evidence to convince someone else to seek it on his behalf. And Ezra's word carried about as much weight as the yellow jacket's buzz, only without the sting. The young punk would soon to be off to find his next big fish.

Grant removed the pistol from his back holster and sighted up the hummingbird, knowing it was a ridiculous shot. He squeezed the trigger and fired—pop, pop, pop—and to his surprise the hummingbird went down in the bushes. He walked over and found it scuttling around in the dirt. He'd winged it. A hummingbird with a pistol. Fit for a story. He leaned over and picked up the bird. It wriggled in his hand and stabbed him in the palm with its thin beak, enough to draw blood. He carried it up to the grill and opened the lid. Steam from the wood chips huffed out the smell of apple. He chucked the bird inside and watched its feathers smoke as it hopped pathetically around among the hot irons before succumbing.

But before he could drop the lid, a peculiar feeling overcame Grant. A numbness in his stomach. His neck. The feeling crept up and then throttled him. He felt his eyes bulge and he gasped for breath. His legs gave out and he fell to the patio. He looked up and saw the canopy of palms.

His vision clouded over and he was back in his childhood home, seated on the ground, putting together a building from a mismatched set of Tinkertoys. A comedy record was playing in the background and his father—set with that same notched forehead as his own—was sitting in his chair, watching, smiling. His mother was sprawled on the couch, also watching, her hair curled up in a bun except for a few strays which fell beside her cheeks. *I can't believe how smart our boy is*, said Grant's father. *Someday he's going to be something important. I just know it.* She said, *He definitely got something we don't. But I don't care so much about him being important. I just hope he turns into a decent man.* Grant's father chuckled and with a grunt got up from the chair. *This world*, he said, *don't reward decency*.

Grant felt his father's hands grasp his shoulders for an embrace, but then the memory stopped and once again he was on the patio, shoulders throbbing. He blinked twice. He heard the pop and sizzle of the meat on the grill.

Or was it the rain? Yes. Only a few stray drops, but now thousands, clattering against the patio, wetting his face. He felt emotion inside of him. Was it rain or was he crying? Death, he thought. It makes victims of us all.

TWENTY-TWO

Sybil pulled up the drive toward the mansion with the windows rolled down, even though it was pouring. The smell of rain after a dry spell was like nothing else. It was the smell of hope. She swung around the oval driveway and parked behind Grant's big black sedan. She opened the door of her coupe and the scent hit her in full measure. She breathed in and closed her eyes before stepping out.

She walked to the porch and stood beneath the awning. Grant was probably on the back patio at that very moment, under an umbrella, grilling and plotting some way to exact revenge on the weather for ruining his party. For some reason that image of him made her smile. He was a terrible person and she hated him, but for a moment she left that behind. Maybe it would be like this for a while—her mind slipping into its old habits, her body slipping back into its old sentiments. Or maybe it would always be like that.

She reached into her purse and fingered the thick envelope of initial paperwork that her lawyer had advised her to fill out. Probably the last thing Grant expected was for *her* to present *him* with divorce papers. He'd likely imagined that she'd hold on as long as she could, in the hope that he'd change *his* mind.

It was as though a switch inside of her had flipped in the hotel room, after she'd come to her senses. All of this energy began to prickle through her fingers. She felt so invigorated. It was unbelievable. And she'd had a lot time to think over the last couple of days, because she hadn't slept a bit. Hadn't even felt the need to. It was amazing. She'd called her parents, her old friends. She wrote long to-do lists and filled notebooks with plans. She didn't yet know exactly what she was going to do, but she had a general idea. First, she'd get back into theater. Start from scratch, no company too small. She'd find good parts and play them for free, and trust that the work would be enough to stave off the ridicule she'd surely receive, and the eventual lack of notoriety once folks grew bored of her career change.

Helen's story might be beyond her reach, but there were other stories that needed to be told. When she wasn't acting, she would scour local weeklies, be a student of the stage, get to know writers, travel around the country. She had money. She knew people who had money. She would find projects that needed to be heard, and champion them. She would be someone's angel instead of waiting for one herself. She would work harder than she had ever worked before.

Her inspiration, in some ways—though it angered her to admit it—was Hudson. He had been her angel. A broken, fucked up, arrogant, deceptive angel, but still . . . she doubted she could've gotten as far without his help. She knew that she owed him nothing, but her feelings—as always—betrayed her. She figured the only way to get rid of that guilt was by helping others, but without making the same demands he'd imposed on her. It would be perfect payback for the ways in which she had, through Grant, benefited at others' expense.

And once she felt settled, she would begin searching for love. She wanted a companion. Ezra would never take her back, and she couldn't trust that she really wanted him, anyway. He was a fling—but that didn't mean it wasn't meaningful, and that she hadn't learned from it. She was still figuring out what it meant to be this Sybil Harper. But when the time came, she wouldn't wait for someone to find her. She'd go after it with the same abandon that she had her career.

This energy was strange. She knew it couldn't last—she'd need sleep sometime—but she took it as a sign. She'd done the right thing, going off the medications, sleeping with Ezra, sabotaging things with Grant, ending this episode of her career. Her body seemed to know it, as did her mind. The future seemed to spread out before her, glowing.

She felt nothing short of fantastic.

She took her keys from her purse and jingled them around until she found the one. She slid it into the keyhole and was a tad surprised that it still fit. Grant hadn't bothered to change the locks. Cocky bastard. She went inside and was met with the familiar smell of what had been her home. It tugged at her. Sorrow. Regret.

"Grant?" No reply. She peered into the foyer and walked through. The lights were on in the kitchen and there were plates of vegetables already prepared, empty highball glasses waiting to be filled. He'd lined up some red wines, even popped a few open and poured them into decanters to breathe. "Hello?"

She glanced out the patio doors and saw that the grill was closed and cooking. Grant was probably in the restroom or in his office making phone calls. She left the kitchen and hopped up the stairs. "Are you here?"

The master bedroom looked much as she'd left it, though she could smell other perfume. He'd had women here. No surprise. Hopefully they weren't still here. She'd rather not see them if she could help it. "Grant?"

She stepped into the large arcade that housed the paneled oriel window, looked out on the grounds, and almost fainted. Before her was what she'd seen in all of those dreams. Passed out on the patio was Grant, next to the grill, which was sending a plume of steam and smoke up into the palms. She began banging on the window. "Grant!" she screamed. "Grant!"

He didn't move. She ditched her heels and ran from the room and down the spiral staircase, almost slipping on the last few steps, then sprinted as fast as she could through the hall and kitchen. She thrust open the patio doors and rushed to his side.

"Grant." She slapped his cheeks. They were hollow and ashen. His eyes looked blank. "Grant, honey. Talk to me." She slapped him again. Nothing. She reached to his neck and tried to calm herself enough to feel a pulse. She searched around, digging her fingers into his neck. "No," she said. "No no no."

She knew CPR. She'd had to learn it for a part. She shimmied over to the side of his head and leaned him back and reached into his mouth to make sure that nothing was blocking his airway.

In what was probably only a second, a flood of thoughts filled her mind. Did she actually want to save his life? It could end here. She could call the medics, tell them she'd tried to do CPR and failed. But no, there were cameras; they'd know that was a lie. But couldn't she fake it? Pretend to breathe into his mouth and go through the rest of the motions?

She'd be free to do Helen's movie. She'd get his money and get out from under his wing. Finally do whatever she wanted. There'd be the funeral and events and she could take control of the narrative. She'd be his widow, share in the tragedy and be more respected for it.

If he lived, he'd probably hate her more. He might rather die than have his life saved by someone else, much less her. If he ever regained his senses, he might make her pay for the good she'd done.

He also might not. She couldn't say for certain. Strange that it would be a risk to save a life. But it also could change him into a better man. It was probably the only thing that could.

But as she took in his pale face, all of those questions disappeared. She reached for her phone and dialed 911. She set it next to her and, as she listened to it ring, leaned over and breathed into him.

ACKNOWLEDGMENTS

Thank you to my agent, Reiko Davis at DeFiore & Company, and my editor, Alexandra Hess at Skyhorse Publishing, for helping to shape and bring this book into the world, as well to Mark Pearson at Pear Press for his vision in making the novel an audiobook.

I'm indebted to handful of discerning readers. Miles Wray, Jodi Paloni, Mary Stein, Raymond Fleischmann, Erik Evenson, Robert P. Kaye, and Len Kuntz offered sharp and generous feedback at various stages of the process.

I'm grateful to the Tin House Writer's Conference for their mentorship program and Matthew Specktor for his guidance on revising this book. I'm also thankful for the faculty at Vermont College of Fine Arts, specifically my advisors David Jauss, Nance Van Winckel, Clint McCown, and Abby Frucht.

The following programs and organization provided me invaluable support in completing this book: The Made at Hugo Fellowship through the Hugo House and the Writer's Program at the Jack Straw Cultural Center, both in Seattle.

I could not have finished this book without the help of my family, whom I depended on for strength and backing throughout.

Finally, thank you to my wife, Jess. Your patience and kindness sustain me.